ASHES TO MURDER

A JILL QUINT, MD SERIES NOVEL

ALEC PECHE

ACKNOWLEDGMENTS

You, dear reader asked for this story. I was content to let Nathan and Jill drift along as friends and lovers. However, I heard that you wanted them to marry, so this story is for you.

I'd like to thank GM and Ellen Falk as my editors. You 're able to translate the thoughts I put down on paper to a grammatically correct story. That is no mean feat.

Enjoy,
Alec

Proposal
The violet loves a sunny bank,
The cowslip loves the lea;
The scarlet creeper loves the elm,
But I love—thee.

The sunshine kisses mount and vale,
The stars, they kiss the sea;
The west winds kiss the clover bloom,
But I kiss—thee!

The oriole weds his mottled mate;
The lily's bride o' the bee;
Heaven's marriage ring is round the earth—
Shall I wed —thee?

Bayard Taylor, 1859

CHAPTER 1

*J*ill Quint, MD, Forensic Pathologist, private investigator, and vintner from California was astounded by this moment in time. Her partner, Nathan Conroy, proposed they get married. She knew they were heading that way, but kudos to the man for arranging the perfect weather and setting. He had placed a lovely engagement ring that he had designed, of course, on her finger. She looked into his blue eyes framed by beautiful black hair and said, "Yes."

They were on a secluded patio attached to their suite over-looking the Blue Ridge Mountains outside of Asheville, North Carolina, in October. Jill had found her requisite sweet white wine while Nathan had a flight of wines in front of him from a local winery. He would be designing their labels in the future, and he always tasted the wine for which he was designing a label.

They toasted their future lives together and spoke more about the actual wedding. They were both in their mid-forties with no children and no plans to create offspring. They had friends and family who would want to witness their nuptials.

"We could get married here on the beautiful grounds of this

hotel. I've got a cocktail party dress with me, but I would probably go into town and shop for something special," Jill said.

"I see no reason to delay our marriage, so let's see if we can get a license, find a place, and locate an officiant. Besides, I told our closest friends and family that I was proposing two weeks ago, so they all planned to come for a long weekend here. Thankfully, you said - yes. Otherwise, I'd be reimbursing a bunch of airfares. We're here for an entire week, so that seems like plenty of time to arrange a simple ceremony and reception. I assumed that is what you would want."

"Wow, they all kept that a secret from me. Congrats on that. Let's get to work arranging that ceremony! That gives us the weekend to enjoy their company."

"Okay, let's spend a moment and put together a small list of invitees beyond those I originally communicated with to see if I left anyone off. We have more friends, like Officer Davis, and maybe we can hold a reception for them when we return to California. Then let's see if we can find a reception room in this hotel. We can go to the courthouse and apply for the license tomorrow, but who should marry us? A judge, or a member of a religious community?"

"Maybe the courthouse has a list of local officiants. It doesn't hurt to ask. The weather is supposed to be good, so we could marry outside somewhere on the grounds here, or we could choose a winery or brewery. We met over wine, so why not marry in a vineyard? Let's go search for a location and an officiant. It will depend on what's available for this Friday, but we'll make it happen," Nathan said with a twinkle in his eye.

"Yes, I'm sure between the two of us, we can get it all planned. Okay, let's go to work."

They started with the hotel concierge. Asheville was a popular place to marry, and many places were already booked. He was able to quickly check some twenty locations.

"Would you like to marry outdoors? I just checked the

weather and rain is not expected on Friday," the concierge asked.

"As we're both involved in the wine industry, is there a vineyard near here that has a unique building that we could use? If not for the reception, at least the wedding?" Jill asked. "If push comes to shove, we can hold a ceremony outdoors and party back in our hotel suite."

The concierge gave some thought to Jill's questions and said, "Maybe."

He then proceeded to click the keys on his keyboard checking something out on the internet. He turned his monitor around so they could see.

"There is a church ruin that is a part of a vineyard that's about thirty miles from here. They are not listed as a banquet space, but perhaps the owner might want to host you. Should I check their availability?"

Jill's blond hair had fallen over her eyes, and she moved it behind her ears to study the picture on the screen and liked the look of the abandoned church. Part of the roof was missing, so there would be sunlight. There was also a vineyard outside of its walls. Given the small party they expected, they calculated they would have perhaps twenty friends and family in attendance. The church ruin could hold both the ceremony and the reception if they could find a caterer.

Jill looked at Nathan, who nodded and said, "It's perfect. Those old windows would make a wonderful backdrop. Can you ask the owner if we can also hold the reception there? We can find a caterer if they don't have a favorite."

The concierge picked up the phone and dialed the vineyard owner. They could only hear his side of the story. It appeared that they could use the grounds for the wedding, but the vineyard owners had no experience with hosting an event like a wedding reception.

After he hung up the phone he said, "The owner has never

been asked if someone can rent out their abandoned church. He wants to do it, but needs to check with his wife and his insurance company. He thinks he'll get back to me within the hour with a price that would include the insurance premium he'll have to pay for the event. He did say there were no bathrooms in the immediate vicinity, but you could bring in some nice porta-potties. You can pick your own caterer, and he said there's parking near the church for your friends."

"We'd like to drive there now to check the site out. Would you ask him if he would mind our doing that? I realize that he hasn't given us permission to go forward, but I do need to see the place in person."

"I'll check; just a moment."

Five minutes later, Nathan and Jill were on the road to the winery, and close to an hour later, they were pulling into Smokey Blue Winery. They had to travel from the south of Asheville through traffic and then east to the vineyard. It was smaller than Jill's winery. A man came from around a building and approached them.

"Hi, I'm Jess Redmond. Are you the couple who want to hold a wedding here on Friday?"

"Yes, we are," Jill said. "I'm Jill Quint and this is Nathan Conroy."

"Congratulations on your nuptials. Let me show you the church ruin and then we can talk about the cost to use this place. There's no reason to discuss cost if the place doesn't suit your needs."

"Indeed," Nathan agreed. They followed Mr. Redmond through a path between the vines. His height was somewhere between Jill's five feet six and Nathan's six feet. He was wearing jeans and a long-sleeve button-down shirt. His ball cap had the logo of the NFL's Charlotte team.

"How did the church end up on your property?"

"It dates back to the Civil War. Many buildings were

destroyed or plundered depending on who was in charge. Typically, buildings were destroyed because they were owned by or housed the soldiers of one side or the other. Historians thought that perhaps the church housed Union soldiers as it was a Presbyterian church that was horrified by slavery. That would be a reason for the Confederates to try and destroy it. I haven't done anything with the building, and it hasn't collapsed any further. The floor is uneven as dirt and debris have blown in over the years."

"Did you plant the vines, or did you buy the vineyard?" Nathan asked.

"I bought the vineyard. It was going to be my retirement job," Jess said.

"How's that going?"

"I've made several discoveries. The previous owner planted the wrong vines for this climate and soil. So, I had to replant. I should be able to bottle my first vintage next summer."

"What grape did you pick?" Jill asked.

"You sound informed about the wine business. I planted Petite Syrah vines. I've also purchased grape juice to play with making a red dessert wine."

"I run a vineyard in California. I've produced a few vintages of Moscato and I've recently expanded into a few new grapes. I'd love to try your red dessert wine."

"If this church works as a site for our wedding, I'd be happy to create a label for your vintages. I'm a wine label designer with about three hundred clients worldwide, including a new client near Asheville."

"Wow, what a day! With where I am in my wine-making career, I can't imagine a more perfect pair to meet than you two."

They came upon the church ruin. Perhaps eighty percent of its roof was intact. There were bars where the window spaces were, but there was something about them that made it decorative rather than having the look of a prison. Jill could see what Jess meant about the floor. They would want to sweep out the debris and flatten the surface, but Jill fell in love with the old church. It had a dignified feeling from the large beige stone walls and would make for a memorable wedding location.

"I love this place. If we had searched high and low for a wedding location, I'm not sure we could have found a better venue. I like the lighting in here and the peace and calm about this old ruin. Jess, you're right that we should do something with the floor. If you can draw up a contract that allows us to bring in someone to fix the floor, rent porta-potties, and hire a caterer, then we'd like to rent this place on Friday for our wedding."

"It is a lovely location," Nathan said. "I would think a small excavator could enter through the doorway and with a few hours' work, clear the floor in here. It's your land and the dirt will have to be dumped somewhere, so we'll leave that up to you. Once we're done, we'll leave you some photos and contact information both to assist you with your wine business and to help you get a wedding venue venture going."

"Wow. While you two were inside looking around, I looked you both up on the Internet. Nathan, I see that you're one of the most sought out wine label artists in the world, and Jill, you seem to be more famous for murder investigations than wine."

Jill smiled and replied, "I lead two lives. In one life I make great Moscato wine. In the other life, I'm a forensic pathologist who has helped bring bad people down around the world. Nathan has been at my side for most of those adventures as I often come too close to the killer. When we first started dating I was worried that Nathan wouldn't want to date someone who finds herself in dangerous situations, but he's been very supportive. He's a black belt in Hapkido and has convinced me to start studying Tai Chi. We have a great partnership around wine, friends, and staying alive."

"I'm sorry to keep saying wow, but can I have your life? Sorry dude, I would call off the wedding though. I want you to design my wine labels, but I don't want to marry you."

Nathan chuckled, "I wonder what your wife would say about that?"

"I will have you meet her. She's in Asheville at the moment, but if she doesn't meet you today, I would think you'll be back here to meet with the various consultants you'll need to pull this wedding off in a few days."

"True. Nathan's here to meet with a few wineries regarding his services. That leaves me to do all the work with planning a wedding on short notice. He's more artistic than I am, so maybe I'll put him in charge of the decorations, and I'll handle everything else. Does that sound like a deal, Nathan?"

"I can do that. Are you sure you can handle the remainder? I think we should find the caterer together. What if we can't find a caterer on short notice?"

"I'll exhaust all avenues and if all else fails, I might ask Henrik if we can borrow his cook or something like that."

Nathan raised an eyebrow and said, "That's asking a lot on short notice."

"Do you doubt that he'll change his schedule to attend?"

"Henrik said he would when I gave him a heads up, but I hope we find someone in this area so we don't need to impose on him."

Henrik was a close friend who resided in Germany. He operated one the foremost security and facial recognition companies in the world. Nathan assisted him with a small vineyard in Germany, and Jill had solved his wife's murder several years ago.

"I'm so happy he can join us. Another choice might be to ask Melissa if she could cook for us. I don't know if she can close her winery on short notice, but it's worth a try."

Melissa was a fellow vintner and an excellent cook. She held functions at her winery that were wine and food pairings. She was also a former forensic psychologist.

"We may not have any friends by the end of the reception."

"Ha, I've got very good friends and they'll help me do anything to make our wedding happen. Do you need help with the decorations and flowers?"

"Actually, I was going to fly my assistant here and have him help."

"See, we're both going to do just fine, and we'll end up with a beautiful and memorable wedding in the end."

They arranged a price with Jess Redmond, worked out transferring funds, and set about getting a top-loader in to clean up the church. Jess would also locate porta-potties. A short time later they were on the road and Jill began making calls. She started with her mother in Arizona. Jill was dying to make quick calls, but each person was thrilled for her and wanted details. She was getting anxious with the congratulations and questions from each person. After talking to Angela, she created a group text announcing the ceremony to everyone invited with a promise that she would be calling them to discuss the details.

"Wow," Jill said reading her email. "Henrik's wedding gift to us is a ride for our parents and our friends in Green Bay. What a generous man. When you asked him to attend, he reached out to our friends to offer them one-way plane service as he is leaving here much sooner than anyone else. His pilot needs to find the nearest airports."

"My parents are on the East Coast, so he'll probably want to pick them up before he heads to Wisconsin. I would have him drop everyone off here and then go get your mother from Arizona. Maybe we should just fly her first class here, as I would think she would want to arrive sooner to fuss over you."

"I'll just make introductions and have his pilot contact everyone for details. We'll get married Friday and then everyone can go home on Sunday."

"We're just going to give everyone less than forty-eight hours to celebrate with us and then we'll tell them to get lost?" Nathan said, amused.

"Well, if we were in our twenties and getting married, everyone leaves after the reception, because the bride and groom have gone on a honeymoon. What's so weird about kicking them out after forty-eight hours? You and I both have appointments next week. We need to return home as we planned on Tuesday."

"I guess I don't have to worry about making romantic gestures during our marriage."

"Your proposal was romantic and gave you bonus points in the romance department for many years to come. I, on the other hand, seem to have a negative balance and growing in my romance account."

Nathan reached over for her hand to give it a kiss, "I love you for all your warts and negative romance bank account. You are who you are, and I never worry that I'm in love with a mirage."

CHAPTER 2

Nathan joined Jill in handling the catering, and from a list of caterers, they checked to see who was available that Friday. With three caterers available and the addresses close to Highway 25, they stopped at each. The one they liked best also could provide a wedding cake. With that settled, it was time to find an officiant for the ceremony.

"As I see it, we have three choices; a friend who gets a last-minute certificate to marry us, someone we find online who already has one, or a local religious officiant. We're getting married in an old church and while we don't have an affiliation with any church, I wouldn't mind finding someone affiliated with the Presbyterian church since our ruin was once that. Let's find some local churches and see if we can arrange that as non-members."

"I'm sure our parents would like this given the last-minute nuptials. Not that I care about that, but if we can ease their minds, why wouldn't we? How many Presbyterian churches are in this area?" Nathan asked.

"At least ten. I wonder where we should start?"

"With so many churches, you would think there was an

administrative arm to it. Why don't we start with the biggest or oldest church and go from there?"

They soon found themselves inside a beautiful gothic church looking for someone to help them. After a few questions, they ended up in the church office explaining their problem.

"Are you members of the church?" asked the secretary.

"No. We're getting married in an old church ruin that was a Presbyterian church before it was partially destroyed in the Civil War. We don't have a preference as to who marries us, but we thought we would check with this church given the old church's history."

"Just a moment," the secretary said and left her office.

"They're probably going to say no to us as we aren't members of their church," Nathan said.

"Maybe. Perhaps there is a church elder or minister who loves history and would overlook our lack of affiliation because of our location."

"Perhaps."

They moved on to talk about other wedding details and were surprised when twenty minutes passed before the secretary returned.

"You gave me an interesting question. We would not have allowed you to marry inside our church as you're not affiliated with the Presbyterian religion. However, we do have a layperson who is a history buff. I contacted her to see if she was willing to preside and she said yes. She has her officiant credentials. She'll be a private citizen, not a church-sponsored minister. She knows of the ruin you speak of and would love to see it have a relationship with our church. Perhaps this is a start— those are her words, not mine."

"It might suit the owner's future plans as well, but I won't speculate on that. How do we reach her to discuss the ceremony?"

"She just finished leading a Bible study and will be here in about ten minutes. Once she arrives, I'll leave my office so the three of you can make arrangements."

"Thank you so much for your help. We've been together as a couple for about three years. Nathan proposed this morning and we decided to try and arrange the wedding while we were in Asheville. The concierge at our hotel suggested the ruin. I'm a vintner and Nathan's a wine label artist and we wanted a setting close to a vineyard, but something more, and we found it in that church ruin. We found a caterer; Nathan is doing the decorations as he's more artistic than I am. We wanted to find someone to marry us in this special place. The owner has rented a top-loader to smooth out the inside of the ruin. He'll provide chairs, tables, and fancy porta-potties. We're his first client and he hopes to use the experience to build his business. Sorry, I'm just chattering away about our plans because I'm so excited while I'm probably boring you."

"Actually, I'm enjoying hearing how you came to be connected to the church. We have many pathways, but yours might be the most unique. Maybe Mrs. Locklear will further cement your relationship to our church."

The door opened and a woman walked in much the same age as Nathan and Jill. The secretary stood up, shook their hands, wished them well, and departed.

"Hello, I'm Laura Locklear. I understand you're not a member of our church, but you're looking for an officiant for your wedding this Friday in the old church ruin that's out on the highway east of here. Is that correct?"

"Yes," Jill said. "We have known each other for three years, and Nathan proposed this morning. We're visiting this area from California. We decided to see if we could arrange a wedding by this Friday as we have friends from all over the U.S. and Europe who will be attending thanks to Nathan swearing them to secrecy three weeks before he proposed. So, there is no convenient geographical location for our friends. We've found the perfect location, catering, decorations, license, and a photographer. An officiant was our last piece of the planning. We thought we would start first with this church because, though we are not members, we are marrying inside a Presbyterian church ruin."

"Do you plan to become members of the church after your ceremony?"

Jill looked at Nathan and said, "No."

"Do you believe in God?"

They both nodded. Laura sat quietly thinking about their answers while warring with her desire to see the old church ruin brought to life for their ceremony. As a historian, she could see the irony of the church being destroyed by different groups, not because of their church affiliation, but because of their affiliation to the North or South in the Civil War. Now the church had a chance to return to its spiritual roots through a wedding ceremony. Perhaps, by meeting the owner she could forge a relationship to use the ruin for some church activities. She saw no harm to the church by serving as an officiant, and perhaps some good. So, she decided to preside at their wedding.

"Okay, I'll do the ceremony. Are there particular passages of the Bible you would like read?"

Jill whipped her head toward Nathan, hoping he knew some passages as she couldn't think of one.

"Ecclesiastes 4:9 and Corinthians 13:13. While this is the first marriage for both of us, we're independent people in our mid-forties. Forget any passages about obeying, serving, etc."

Laura laughed at Nathan's responses, "I understand. I'll put together a selection of readings for your ceremony and email it to you. I presume that you might want to write your vows as well?"

Oh no, thought Jill. She could hear the clinking of the cash register as her romance deficit bank account got worse. She looked at Nathan for help.

He smiled at her, understanding her thoughts, and said to the minister, "We don't have them now, but we will on Friday."

Whew, thought Jill. She guessed that Nathan had thought through a few more details than she had for the actual wedding. Maybe it was his marketing background, but he was much better at this stuff than she was.

They confirmed a few more details and Laura asked if she could visit the church on Thursday to see the set-up. They made arrangements to meet on Thursday, shook hands, and left the church.

"Wow, in one dedicated day, we mostly have this planning done. Still on my to-do list are to find a dress and write my vows. Do you have something to wear for the ceremony?"

"I do. I brought a tux with me, hoping you said 'yes.' Do you want your Mom to help you dress shop? We should see how soon we can get her here."

"Actually, I think I'll check in with Marie and Jo as they have more clothes sense than I do. Maybe I can find a dress shop and video call with them."

"I could help you find a dress as well. It's not bad luck to do so," Nathan said.

"It isn't?"

"No. It's a superstition that dates back to the time of arranged marriages when parents were afraid if the groom saw their bride before the wedding, he might not show up. We don't have that worry here. I know who you are and what you look like. I'm heading into this marriage knowing full well that if someone is murdered in the middle of our vows, you would be on the case immediately, wedding be dammed."

"Wow, you're full of wonderful words today. I'm never going to dig myself out of the deficit in the romance department. You have an artist's eye, so I would appreciate your help with a dress. I've been thinking about it and the floor in the church ruin. What would you say to a three-quarter-length ivory dress given my coloring?"

"I think that's an excellent choice. Let's go find it."

The next four days were a whirlwind for Jill and Nathan. They met their officiant at the church ruin on Thursday, and she went over her role; as there were no bridesmaids or groomsmen, there were no reasons to hold a rehearsal dinner. Instead, they gathered for a wine-tasting party as that was all they had time to arrange without knowing their friends' travel arrangements. While many were arriving on Henrik's plane, a few others were making other arrangements.

The noon ceremony rolled around to everyone's delight. Nathan looked dashing in his black tux and silver bowtie and cummerbund. Jill was elegant in a simple ivory satin midi dress with cap sleeves. It was a v-neckline, with a two-inch-wide fabric band at the waistline. If it got cooler, there was a matching jacket she could wear to cover her arms.

The ceremony was simple with its biblical passages, poetry, and the exchange of vows. The weather was perfect. It wasn't so hot that people didn't want to dance, yet it wasn't cool enough to require the attendees to wear sweaters or jackets. The setting was beautiful and Angela handled all of the pictures including some among the fall colors of the area. The catering was excellent – they made good choices and the hot food was hot and the cold was cold. Jill didn't know much about food, but one thing she didn't care for was a dish in a temperate range that suited neither hot nor cold food. The caterer had even lined up a DJ for the reception and their group had a great time dancing to both 80's pop music and Motown hits.

Nathan's assistant did a beautiful job with the decorations. The church ruin looked dignified and serene like it had woken up from a century-long nap to house the beauty of Nathan's and Jill's wedding. There was no electricity, so his assistant lit the interior with tapered candles and used grapevines and ribbons in the decorations. Other than her small bridal bouquet, they elected to avoid flowers in large part due to the planning time being so short. The caterer brought a generator that was left outside to power her hot dishes and the DJ had a battery-powered unit. The chairs were simple white folding chairs that their guests later moved to eat at the circular tables placed in another corner of the ruin. There was a scent of burning candles and earth from the freshly smoothed floor.

As far as Jill and Nathan were concerned, their wedding could not have been better if they had spent months planning it. It was simple and elegant and now they were man and wife. They were the last to leave and took a moment to enjoy the silence after the solemnity of the day.

"Dr. Quint, or Mrs. Conroy, ah I need your help," Jess Redmond said, as he rushed into the ruin.

"What's wrong?" Jill asked, having her wedding happy bubble burst. The fact that he called her by her title meant that something was wrong medically.

"Mrs. Locklear is lying in one of the grapevine rows and I can't rouse her."

Oh, no, Jill thought running outside just behind Jess. The soil wasn't meant for her heels, but she needed to see what happened to their officiant.

They arrived at where Jess was standing to indeed see their officiant lying on the soil and not moving. She looked like she'd fallen asleep on the soil in the sunshine. Jill reached down and felt for a pulse, looking at her watch. She felt the woman's skin to judge its temperature. She looked at her eyes and saw clouded corneas. She made the decision not to start resuscitation. She looked at her watch and thought back to when she had last seen Mrs. Locklear.

"I think I saw Laura disappear once she'd taken the time to meet our attendees not long after the reception began. Which was about three hours ago. Jess, call 9-1-1 to report a death. I don't see a reason to perform CPR as she's been dead a while."

Jess made the call, and Jill said to Nathan, "I'm sorry."

"You're apologizing because you plan to get involved with this death on our wedding night in your wedding dress. That's who I married. If this death is ruled a homicide, you'll get justice for Laura Locklear; and as I enjoyed her as our officiant, you'll be doing that for me as well. We're okay."

"I love you, Nathan Conroy. Thank you for understanding that if this death is ruled a homicide, I'll get involved and find justice for Laura as she deserves that from me."

"I love you, Jill Quint. Is there anything I can get for you? I could return to the hotel for some clothing and different shoes for you."

"You're the best, but I had a feeling my feet would hurt in time in these heels, so there's a bag in our rental car with flat shoes; if you could fetch those, that's all I need at this time."

"The police should be here in about fifteen minutes. As you can imagine, there isn't a local station. They are sending an ambulance as well. What should we do? Should we put a blanket on her or make her more comfortable?"

Jill felt bad for Jess Redmond. He was seeing his business dreams take off with this day's wedding, but then to find a young woman dead in his vineyard was a shock. Most people went through an entire life without coming upon a dead person.

She put her hand on his arm and said, "It's okay, Jess, she's at peace and she's comfortable at the moment. We don't want to touch her or move her as we may be tampering with evidence that she's left us."

"Evidence? Evidence of what?"

"From a law enforcement perspective, a young woman like Laura shouldn't be dead. I don't know her medical history, but I didn't notice any obvious health condition the few times I met with her. If I were the medical examiner called to this scene, this would be a suspicious death."

"Oh my gosh, I don't know what to say or do."

"There's nothing you can do. The experts will be here shortly, and they'll take it from there. The only thing for us to do is not contaminate this scene."

Nathan returned with her flat shoes, which Jill changed into and Nathan took her high heels back to the car. He also brought the jacket that matched her dress as it was dusk and October, so the temperature would drop to fifty overnight. He was returning to Jill's side when they saw flashing lights in the distance and the sound of a siren. It was, hopefully, a cavalry coming to the scene.

"Do you want to go to your driveway and direct the group to park near the church?" Jill asked Jess.

He looked relieved to have something to do and he took off toward his house.

"I'll go to our parking area and bring the officer here so you can stand guard over Laura. I dug your cellphone out of your purse in case you want to take any pictures."

"You're the best, anticipating my needs," Jill said, then looked down at the woman and wondered why she was dead.

Within twenty minutes, they had plenty of spectators from fire, police, and an ambulance crew. Mostly Jill thought, because the story was so strange. She could imagine the headline in the newspaper, 'Officiant Dead after Wedding or Reception Kills Officiant,' ugh.

A detective arrived along with investigators who set up crime scene lighting given the impending dusk and took pictures. Jess, Jill, and Nathan were all separately interviewed. It was weird when each party congratulated them on their wedding and then moved on to questions about the dead woman who had so recently pronounced them married.

Jill inwardly smiled when she heard someone checking her

credentials as a forensic pathologist and P.I. Her licenses and experiences were validated. She was glad they checked her background—it was good police work.

"Do you think this is a homicide?" Detective James Parnell asked when he finished questioning her about the scene.

"Really, Detective, there's not enough evidence yet to label this as anything other than a suspicious death. I haven't even seen her backside to determine if her head was bashed, or her neck broken. I see no obvious gun or knife wounds. She could have overdosed, I suppose. I've determined that she had no pulse or respiration and was well beyond the period when CPR might have helped. She teaches Bible studies at the gothic Presbyterian church in Asheville. Her name is on our wedding license, and I don't know much more about her other than she was an excellent officiant at our wedding. She was in good health with no noticeable pain or breathing problems. I'd offer to assist with her autopsy, but I don't have a license in this state, and I have a conflict of interest. I would be happy to provide my expert opinion if asked."

"I'll pass it on. The victim is heading to Charlotte when we're done here as we don't have nearby forensic services in Asheville. Who introduced you to her?"

Jill explained about the wedding on short notice in a Presbyterian church ruin and her conversation with the church secretary in town. "All I can say is I didn't notice that she had any obvious medical problems—she wasn't short of breath and walked with a good gait. Someone who is ailing doesn't do those things."

She broke off her explanation when the investigative team got ready to move her. She returned to Laura's side but didn't notice anything that might have gotten the woman killed. She was loaded onto a litter and carried over to an ambulance gurney at the end of the parking lot. She was placed inside, the doors were slammed shut, and the ambulance set off on its one-hundred-mile journey to Charlotte. Jill turned her glance to where Laura had lain in the dirt but saw nothing that caught her eye. She took a few pictures which the detective frowned about.

"This is a crime scene, and you shouldn't take pictures."

"When we return to the hotel, my team and I will go to work on this case. I need pictures to explain the scene."

The detective sighed and was about to say something but then must have realized he would be wasting his breath.

The investigators would spend a little more time before departing. Jill and Nathan returned to their rental car to head to their hotel once they were released by the detective, having left their contact information with him.

CHAPTER 3

"This is a unique wedding night. I didn't expect, though I probably should have, to have a death as the grand finale to our ceremony," Nathan said.

"Ditto. We must have some strange karma that whenever our group is together, dead bodies pop up. We'll have to group text everyone with the news as I suspect that everyone is leaving us alone tonight."

"So what is your guess as to what happened?"

"Like I told the detective, she had no obvious medical issues. She walked with speed; she spoke in full sentences, which indicates she wasn't short of breath. There was no quiver in her voice as she married us. She's too young to have a heart attack. She could have an aneurysm in the brain or aorta. However, she should have had a headache and she wasn't frowning in pain or rubbing her head."

"Wow, you really observe people," Nathan mused.

"Habit. She could be a drug overdose, but I didn't notice weird pupils, bad teeth or skin, or other signs of drug use. She had no reason to walk in the vineyard. After she left our reception, I would have thought she would drive back to town. Her car was in the opposite direction of the vines. She saw the vine-yard the other day and I can't recall a special interest from her in viewing the vines."

"Do you think this will be murder?"

"Probably."

"What was Jess doing in the area?"

"Our reception was over, and he was coming by to see if he needed to do anything when he noticed her lying in the dirt, one row over. At this time of year with fewer leaves and no grapes on the vines, he must have caught a glimpse of her. Human nature was to leave the ruin and turn left to head to the parking lot, and besides you wouldn't pass the row she was lying in," Jill said.

"Are you satisfied with the cops?"

"Too soon to tell. They didn't have a bad technique in collecting evidence from the crime scene that I observed, but let's see how they go about collecting additional evidence and interviewing people. I heard them checking my credentials which was a wise move."

"Of course, there's the upcoming autopsy which is really where you like to add your two cents' worth."

"I know. I've been trying to think of a way to wiggle in to observe it, but I haven't thought of anything so far."

"Such bridal thoughts," Nathan said with a grin.

"Hey, you married me knowing what my bridal warts might be. You just didn't expect to have them validated so soon."

"True, and I love you anyway. If examining a dead body is your idea of a great time on your wedding night, have at it; we have the rest of our lives to get further acquainted. I've got your back."

"I love you, too, for your unconditional support. My romance department bank account is so overdrawn, I don't know if I'll ever break even, let alone have some currency in it.

Let me put a word into the ear of the lead investigator to see if I can get anywhere."

She left a voicemail on the detective's line reminding him of her expertise and the desire to observe the autopsy. She also put a call into the Charlotte branch of the State Medical Examiner to see if she could get an invite that way. They pulled up to the hotel and sent a group text to Angela, Marie, Jo, and Henrik asking them to meet them on their terrace for drinks and a death discussion in half an hour after explaining what happened after they left. The replies were everything from *OMG* to *of course that would happen at your wedding*. They changed their clothes and ordered snacks and wine to be sent up, and they were ready to receive their friends.

"This is so weird. This is supposed to be your wedding night and here we all are crowding into your suite," Jo said. "It's the one night of your lives where you don't want company."

"Really, though, shouldn't we have expected this? Almost every time we get together as a group some crime occurs that we must solve. The gods must want us to exercise our brains this way," Henrik said. "Give us the details and we'll go from there."

Just then Jill's phone rang with the Charlotte area code she was waiting for. She mentioned that to the group then stepped into the bedroom to talk. She returned a few minutes later to dead silence. Clearly, everyone was waiting for her to talk.

"That was the Charlotte Medical Examiner's Office. They see me as having a conflict of interest as I am rightly a suspect at this moment, so I can't attend the autopsy, but they did ask me about my thoughts, so I like that they seem to be operating under good principles."

"What did you advise them to do?" Marie asked.

"I told them why I thought it was going to be ruled a homicide, and gave them a rundown of what I would look for if I was doing an autopsy. That was about as much as I could expect from their office."

"Why are you a suspect?" Angela asked.

"Actually, all of us are suspects. We were all at the last place Laura Locklear was seen alive."

"Do you think I am free to leave the United States?" Henrik asked.

"If the police show up shortly and start taking everyone's statement, I think you would be free to leave. If they don't show up soon, then you're still free to leave as there is nothing stopping you," Jill said with a shrug.

"Should you give that warning to all the wedding guests?" Marie asked.

"Yes, we probably should," Nathan said. "I'll take care of that right now. Anything I should tell people about this investigation?"

"Let's tell them the police have a list of attendees at the wedding. If they have any pictures of the officiant, they should plan to turn them over, and if they can think about the last time they saw her, that would be good," Jill said.

Nathan nodded and typed away. "I'll step away and handle any calls or texts from our guests."

Marie brought her laptop and began looking for information on their victim. Angela started scrolling through the hundreds of pictures she took, copying any photos of Laura into a new folder. Jo decided to investigate the local Presbyterian church to see if its finances were on solid ground. Henrik had nothing to do as there were no security issues and no need for his facial-recognition software as they knew everyone at the wedding. Then he thought of someone who needed researching.

"Angela, why don't you send me pictures of the catering crew? Weren't they the only strangers at the wedding?"

"That's brilliant, Henrik! Yeah, if you would research them, then we will have everyone covered," Jill said.

"What are you working on, Jill?" Marie asked.

"I'm creating a list of what could be the murder weapon. I didn't see any blood. Her neck could have been broken, or she was poisoned, is all I can think of. I wish I could participate in the autopsy, but when they bring someone to trial later, having me in the autopsy suite might create problems for the prosecutor."

"You could contact her husband, explain your background and experience, and ask to do an autopsy gratis," Marie suggested.

"That's a thought. So, she's married. Are there any children?"

"No. She's been married for about a decade. Her husband is a minister in the church. Oh, his social media account says he's at a church retreat in Tennessee. He's not at home for you to approach and I'd advise against doing a cold call on the phone."

"I have to agree with you there. How long has the husband been there?"

"All week. He's in Nashville which is about a five-hour drive from here."

"He could have made that drive, murdered his wife, and been back in Nashville before the police located him to notify him of Laura's death. You always suspect the husband first," Jill said.

"Did you pay her for being your officiant?" Jo asked.

"Yes. We gave her a check on Thursday. It's not likely that Nathan and I would kill her in order to save money on our wedding. If that were the case, it would be easier for us to fly to Las Vegas. Besides, that doesn't get us out of the location rental or the cost of the catering."

Marie looked up from her computer and said, "Maybe the caterers are next."

"Should Nathan and I just go turn ourselves in now?" Jill asked with a laugh.

"We're just prepping you for future interviews with the

police," Angela said from where she was studying the photographs she'd taken.

"Thanks, guys. This has to be one of the strangest wedding nights ever," Jill said. "Henrik remarked earlier that whenever we gather as a group, murder seems to happen, and we should have expected someone to die. That's really a creepy thought."

"Yes, but it's mostly true. I think the only time we did not have a murder was the Green Bay Packers football game I flew in for. Perhaps there was enough violence on the field for the gods to be satisfied that day," Henrik said.

"Yes, I'm sure that's the explanation," Marie agreed.

"So, what are our next steps?" Henrik asked. "I gave all the caterer staff information to Marie so she can add it to the other people she's investigating. In watching American television, I believe our next step is to find a motive, and we don't have one yet. We have a nice average woman, in good health, who died from unexpected causes. Since she and her husband are both connected to the church, what's going on there, Jo?"

"It's rather surprising given all the Presbyterian churches in this area, but financially they are in a lot of trouble. They've been saved temporarily by the loans the government gave out to small businesses to help them weather the pandemic. They're not taking in enough contributions from their members to keep all the churches functioning. The congregations don't appear to be that large, and they should probably consolidate locations. Give me a little more time and I'll see if there's anything else odd about their books."

"We need a religious expert to talk to about Presbyterian behavior. Do they have a confession process? Do they counsel couples about to wed inside their churches? Have they had an altar boy scandal, etc.? Who has that skill?" Jill asked.

Nathan returned to their area, his calls having been made, and heard Jill's question. "How about the secretary in the church who suggested Laura? I bet she would help us understand her church's processes."

"Excellent point, Nathan. She did seem like a friendly sort and she's likely an acquaintance of Laura given how she arranged the meeting and knew that she had her officiant license," Jill said. "I think that you or I will have to question her, though. Why don't we go first thing in the morning and try to find her at the church? Surely the church knows by now of her death as the police would have contacted the husband and he would have relayed the information to the church."

"A few of our guests, including your mother, would like to join us in solving this murder mystery. What should we do? Our wedding night is starting to feel like one of those cheesy murder mystery dinners where everyone tries to solve a murder."

Jill stared at Nathan at a loss for words. "They want to help? What kind of skills do they have to help us?"

"It's your mother, I'm not going to say anything about any skills that she does or doesn't have. I put off my parents and my brother. We could call Melissa in for help," Nathan said and then added for the rest of the group, "Melissa owns a vineyard about an hour or so from Jill's vineyard. She's a former criminal psychologist and was helpful with Jill's arson case, but I'm not sure we have any facts for her to chew on."

"True," Jill said, somewhat dazed at how the day had changed and the fact that many of their wedding attendees wanted to help with a murder case.

Marie could tell that Jill was having trouble organizing her thoughts in her usual efficient manner. She thought she probably could help.

"Nathan, do you have a large sketchbook with you?"

"Yes. Do you need a few sheets?" Nathan replied, catching on to Marie's plan.

"Let's put four sheets together for Jill's murder board. I'll run down to the lobby desk and scrounge up some tape. Then we can write things down and think about the next steps. Isn't that what you usually do, Jill?"

"It is. I'm just so discombobulated from this week of planning a wedding, celebrating my marriage to Nathan, finding a dead woman, and then learning that our friends and family want to help. It's made me lose my mind."

"So what would you want to do?" Nathan asked.

"I guess we should continue the wedding celebration in the suite and get everybody's thoughts on suspects and motives. I think I'm going to need some cake and alcohol to manage the next few hours."

Jill got a few hugs from friends while Nathan went to work trying to find cake and additional wine glasses for everyone. It had been at least three hours since the caterers had packed up their stuff, but he knew his bride would think better on a sugar high. Nathan's job in any case was to protect Jill and keep her fed well while her brain went to work on the problem. So he got to it.

CHAPTER 4

The suite was hot and noisy with all the people chattering about the murder. Fortunately, the evening had cooled down from the day and the open door to their patio had fresh air circulating in the room. Jill took a moment to set her board up and then had Marie add everything they knew about their victim, Laura Locklear. Jo added her piece about the church. Then Jill went to work on a list of suspects that included everyone in the room. Then she added the husband and the information that Henrik had collected on the catering staff.

There was a knock on the suite door and Nathan expected that it was the food he had ordered from room service and hoping they had managed to scrounge up a cupcake for Jill. Instead, when he opened the door, Detective James Parnell stood there. With cop eyes, he took in what looked to be a murder mystery party and frowned.

Nathan stepped in his path and said, "Mate, don't make a fool of yourself. You have one of the best murder investigators in the world on this case. She's dealing with friends and family

"""

who want to help. No one is amused by the situation, least of all me. What do you need from us?"

The detective glanced across the room at the sketch paper on the wall with the facts the wedding party collected since he last spoke with them. Silence fell on the group as Jill realized who had stepped inside. She'd met the detective, but the others hadn't.

"Detective Parnell, how can I help you?" Jill asked.

"Mr. Conroy assures me that this is not a 'Murder on the Orient Express Mystery party.' I need to interview probably all the people in this room if you were at the wedding today."

He then took a moment to read what was on the paper and he was amazed this group had collected more information than he had. Still, he couldn't help but ask, "Who are you people?"

"Detective, I believe I gave you my card. Some of the people in this room are a part of my normal team that has solved perhaps twenty or thirty murders in the United States, Canada, Italy, Belgium, Scotland, and Down Under. We are assembling the facts on this case and trying to solve what I suspect will eventually be labeled as a homicide. An injustice was done to the kind woman who performed our nuptials and we won't let that go unsolved."

"Dr. Quint, I've been on the case for a few hours. You make assumptions that this is a homicide and further that my department will be unable to solve it. We are not incompetent," the detective said tightly.

"I don't assume that you are. I just see no reason not to provide the professional assistance of me and my team when we are right here at the scene of the crime."

"You may have contaminated witness statements for me by discussing memories within this group."

"I may, but we haven't discussed in this room what everyone saw. Rather, we've collected the time stamp photos that Laura Locklear is in, and we have investigated her background and that of her husband. We've just moved on to the church's finances. I haven't asked a single person in this room what they saw. Would you like to use the outdoor patio to interview everyone in this room?"

He let out a sigh and said, "I'm going to ask a fellow officer to sit in on your discussion to make sure that what witnesses saw is not discussed, and I'll interview outside." He looked at the room of about ten people and rubbed his forehead over the situation. He could tell this case was going to be a headache for him and perhaps his department. This woman was royalty in the forensic pathology world, and she was going to interfere with the case.

"Okay, send your officer over." Jill reached into her purse to pull out some things that hadn't made it with her to the church. She said to the detective, "Here's my PI License, my Board certification in forensic pathology and toxicology, and about five law enforcement agencies' business cards that you can contact to check the work of this team. Feel free to take a picture of these documents," laying them out on the table in the room.

Nathan was leaning against the wall both pained and amused by the situation. His new bride was completely ignoring their wedding night to chase her passion of bringing justice to victims of homicides. The detective that he had warned at the door was now overwhelmed by Jill's control of information concerning his case. Oh well, he knew what he was getting into when he proposed marriage. He was attracted to her relentless pursuit of justice even when she put it above their relationship, or it put it above her or their safety.

"How did you get so much information collected on the catering crew and our victim so quickly?" the detective asked.

Jill pointed to Marie and said, "Marie's a social media detective. In her day job, she prepares dossiers on people seeking employment, and seeing what they've said or posted on social media tells you something about the person. It may not be something that affects their employment, but then again, the information may give you warning lights that this person is going to be a problem."

"A social media detective? What kind of California speak is that?" the detective scoffed.

"I live and work in Wisconsin and I have a second house and family in Raleigh. I believe that social media detective is North Carolina speak," Marie said.

The detective had no comeback for Marie's comment, so instead, he asked how they found the catering people's names so quickly. "I can't imagine that you collected a full name for everyone at the wedding."

Henrik said, "I'm Henrik Klein, CEO of Klein Industries based in Stuttgart, Germany. My company provides software for security worldwide including several programs used by many law enforcement agencies in the United States. Perhaps you have used some of them." He then gave the detective a list of programs that the detective used or had wanted to use. "I have a facial recognition program that identified the catering staff in the pictures that Angela took. She has about four hundred pictures of the wedding and video as well," he said gesturing to Angela.

The detective folded at that point. He was dealing with a knowledgeable group and he was glad that the gentleman at the door had stopped him from making a fool of himself, as he had planned to castigate them. These people were serious about finding their murder suspect, and they had serious skills and technology to do so. It was going to be a long night as he collected statements and evidence from them. He also needed to follow up on the bride's business cards. She had two different FBI offices to serve as a reference. He didn't think he'd ever come across a witness with so many resources to help him solve a crime. He decided that he wanted to leave the team for last to interview. He pointed to an older woman who seemed to be on her own and asked, "Who are you and let me interview you first."

"I'm Barbara Quint, Jill's mother. I'm not part of her team and I likely don't have anything relevant to add compared to others in this room."

"Ma'am, I'll make this quick. Let's step outside while I take your statement."

Jill could tell her mom was thrilled to take part in her small role in this mystery. She'd be talking about her daughter's wedding for months and years to come as it was so unusual. She smiled at her encouragingly as her mom and the detective stepped outside.

They were outside for less than ten minutes, and then the detective selected Nathan's parents and brother, and finally Nathan.

"Thank you for stopping me from putting my foot in my mouth. That would have hindered my information collection if I had started out that way."

"Over our years together, I've watched Jill interact with law enforcement all over the world, and you wouldn't have been the first detective to try and blow her up. Those other officers and detectives lived to regret their behavior, and it slows down a case when people have to stumble over their egos. She wants justice for Laura Locklear, nothing more, nothing less. She could have helped your coroner wherever he or she is located, as she has performed thousands of autopsies. You may think of getting her invited to observe the one for Laura."

"On your wedding night?"

"I knew what I was getting into when I proposed marriage. I've watched her put me second many times during the period we've been dating as she seeks justice for a victim or the family left behind. That passion is very sexy. I occasionally contribute to her cases as an outsider civilian, but mostly I keep her and her team fed and hydrated. I also have a black belt and provide security on occasion."

The detective then began detailed questioning as to how Nathan knew Laura Locklear.

"We planned our wedding in four days. It was an amazing feat. Our hotel concierge recommend the old church ruin and we liked it as soon as we saw it. We lined up a caterer and a landscaper to clean up the ruin. The vineyard owner found some nice porta-potties and we were set for most everything except someone to officiate our wedding. We went to the big Presbyterian church in Asheville to see if there might be interest from someone since the old church was, at one time, Presbyterian. Because we are not members of that faith, nor do we plan to be, the church did not want to supply us with a minister. We understood their position. However, the church secretary called Laura as she knew Laura had recently officiated at another wedding. She came over to the church and we discussed our needs and she agreed to officiate. We also met her at the venue yesterday so she could see the ruin and the setup. She was a history buff she said. Today she arrived before our ceremony, married us, stayed around for perhaps half an hour of the reception, and then she left. She knew no one from our wedding other than Jill and me, but she was gracious to our guests. There were no locals at our reception. She was fascinated by the church ruin. She rubbed her hands over different parts of it as she was feeling for the life the walls had experienced. The next time I saw her was where you found her, lying between the vineyard rows."

"Where were you when Jess Redmond notified you that she was dead?"

"He didn't say she was dead. He said she wasn't responding to his voice. We had just finished our final look around the reception area to make sure that no one left anything behind. Jill rushed over to see if she could do anything, but she could tell that Laura had been dead for a while, so we asked Jess to call the police. We knew it would take you at least fifteen to twenty minutes to get there, and so we kept watch over her while we waited for help."

"After you left the vineyard, when did you gather everyone to start work on this case?"

"We texted them on the way back to this hotel, and so they were waiting for our arrival. We changed out of our wedding finery and Jill went to work while I kept everyone hydrated and fed. That's the useful skill I bring to these cases," Nathan said with a wry smile. "Oh, and I also keep the killer away from Jill and her friends."

"Do you carry a weapon with you?"

"No. As I mentioned earlier, I am a Master black belt in Hapkido. My hands and feet are my weapons."

The detective took a minute to write some notes and then said, "Thanks. The two of you have an unusual collection of friends, especially the CEO of Klein Industries."

"Yes, they are amazingly helpful. Henrik has been a great friend since Jill solved his wife's murder several years ago. He has an amazing home outside of Stuttgart that contains a training area for police teams from all over Europe."

"Would you send those friends out one by one starting with Mr. Klein?"

Nathan nodded and returned inside, sending Henrik outside with encouraging words: "This is probably your first and last opportunity to be an actor in an American Crime TV show."

"I'll remember to tell my German friends when we all appear on the big screen," Henrik replied as he exited the room. Angela was next and was outside for quite some time, probably being asked about her pictures and videos. Jo was next; the detective hadn't realized she went to work gathering financial information on the church and the victim. He continued to be amazed at how much information this group of amateur sleuths had managed to gather in a short time. Marie followed and then Jill was last.

He started with some of the same questions he'd asked Nathan about where they met the victim. He then moved on to what she observed when Jess Redmond called her to the vineyard.

"She was lying somewhat on her side back in a comfortable position. Her eyes had glazed. I noted no visible wounds or blood in the soil around her. I checked her pulse which as I expected was absent. Her corneas had started to glaze over. I then felt her skin to judge her body temperature and determined that CPR would be fruitless. I asked 9-1-1 to be called to report a death."

"A death and not a homicide?"

"C'mon detective. As a forensic pathologist, I had too little information to make any determination other than dead or alive."

"Yet later when I spoke to you, you thought it would be labeled homicide. Why the change?"

"Your people had turned her over. I could then see no wounds in the back or an unnatural angle to her neck. I had two meetings plus the wedding to observe the victim. She exhibited no signs of acute illness that would result in her death in just hours. She wasn't looking nauseated or in pain which precede heart attacks, strokes, or aneurysms. She read passages from the Bible barely drawing a breath. She's young, she moved with vigor. People like that just don't drop dead two hours after you last saw them. In my mind, that eliminates a natural death.

"She could have died from an accident, but I saw nothing around her indicating that she might have broken her neck in a fall. So that leaves suicide, which would quickly be determined by your medical examiner. Again, she didn't strike me as someone in acute mental distress. She didn't shoot herself, or slash her wrists, or try to drown herself. That leaves pills, but I watched your team sort through the contents in her purse and there was no medication bottle. So suicide is highly unlikely at this point.

"She could be labeled an undetermined, but frankly that would mean you have a crappy medical examiner and I doubt that is the case. So that brings me to homicide. Judging by the lack of vomit nearby, I would guess it was an anesthetic drug or a paralytic."

The detective continued to write notes after Jill finished her discussion. His phone made a beeping sound and he looked at it.

"Would you like to join me at the autopsy of Laura Locklear? It will begin in an hour to give me time to get there. I can give you a ride there and back."

"I'd love to join you. She was a nice person; she made our wedding memorable and perfect. We need to find out why she is dead."

"I sent the medical examiner your credentials and they invited you as an observer. It seems you have a positive reputation in your profession."

"I do mostly. There was a case in San Francisco that forever put me on the Forensic Pathologist map."

"Let's leave now and you can answer some more questions on our way."

CHAPTER 5

*J*ill changed into protective overalls so that she wouldn't leave any DNA behind in the autopsy room. The detective likewise had an enormous white fabric jumpsuit over his work clothes. The suits were nicknamed "bunny suits" as wearers tended to look like a bunny minus the floppy ears and bushy tail when they wore such a suit. They entered the autopsy suite to find the medical examiner and an autopsy assistant ready to begin. Their names were entered into the record, as well as the victim's vital statistics—height, weight, age, probable ethnicity, and more dry facts about Laura Locklear. Dr. Holly Baker was conducting the examination.

"Would you mind if I follow behind you while you examine the skin?" Jill asked Dr. Baker.

"Why don't I follow you?" replied Dr. Baker. Jill shrugged, and began her examination, placing what looked like a jeweler's eyepiece over one eye.

"What position was she in when you found her?" Dr. Baker asked.

"She was partially on her left side. She had her knees drawn up slightly as though she decided to lie down on the dirt and take a nap. Unfortunately, it was the nap of all eternity. She didn't look like she was dropped to the ground or pushed. She simply looked like she was sleeping," Jill said, pointing out marks on Laura's skin. Mostly, they were old scars and a bruise that hadn't turned yellow yet. Jill found no puncture or ligature marks. She finished one side and then they turned her over. Jill found nothing remarkable.

"Still think this is a homicide?" asked Detective Parnell.

"I do. My reasoning still works."

"So, what killed her?"

"We don't know yet. Are you always this impatient? Let's examine her major organs as that may yield new information. Dr. Baker, have you received any labs yet on our victim?"

"Not yet, but we expect the first results back within the next thirty minutes. We don't have a lab here in this facility, but our staff walked our blood samples over to the University lab across the street. As you know, some tests are special, and it will take days to weeks to get the results back. Tonight, we should get chemistry, toxicology, and some organ function tests back."

Dr. Baker proceeded with the autopsy, making incisions and weighing organs. They examined the stomach contents and it included the partially digested food from the wedding. Jill thought that most humans would vomit if they viewed the partially digested food that they recently served someone, but she was interested from the viewpoint that there were no pills in her stomach suggesting an overdose.

The mortuary assistant announced that some test results had arrived.

"The victim has some abnormal chemistry and she's positive for fentanyl."

"What's the level?" Jill asked.

"10ng/ml."

"Sounds like we have a fentanyl fatality. How did she get the fentanyl? I didn't see any needle marks and nothing in her stomach. Could it be a transdermal patch, or perhaps she smoked or inhaled it?" Jill asked the room.

"There were no patches on her body when she was brought in and nothing in her purse. There wasn't a lighter or matches. We'll get her medical history over the next few days," the mortuary technician said.

"So, this will be labeled as an accidental overdose?" Detective Parnell asked.

Jill didn't want to speak for Dr. Baker, so she let the pathologist answer.

"No. At this point, the cause of death is pending. It's odd that someone would overdose on fentanyl but have no evidence of how they would consume it. We have no indication of a needle or pill, so that leads me to think about a patch, but how do you pull the patch off after you're dead? Or if she inhaled it, where's the mask, or cigarette lighter? I have seen overdoses by those methods before, but the evidence was always alongside the body."

"I've never seen someone die from a fentanyl overdose who had managed to pull the patches off and dispose of those patches beyond the vicinity of where he or she died," Jill said.

"I'll send a team out to the vineyard tomorrow to look for the patch. Can you tell if she was a regular fentanyl user?"

"Not necessarily. We'll check her urine for the drug, which will indicate if it was in her system for one to two days," Dr. Baker said.

The mortuary technician called out, "Urine negative for fentanyl."

"She has no obvious injuries or recent surgeries that would call for pain relief. She could have a chronic condition like fibromyalgia that we can't see in our examination so far," Jill said. "When are you interviewing her husband? He should be able to answer some of the questions this autopsy raises."

"I have a partner interviewing him now as he should have returned from Nashville. Let me make sure they ask some of these questions," the detective said, stepping out of the autopsy suite.

"What do you think, Dr. Quint?" Dr. Baker asked.

"I think you'll eventually label this case as a homicide."

"Because . . . ?"

"I observed the victim several times over the past week. I saw no signs of addiction, no signs of a chronic painful condition that would put her in anything but good health. Her liver isn't damaged from chronic use and urine didn't contain the drug, indicating that she hadn't used it in the last few days other than at the time of her death. There is no evidence that she injected or swallowed the drug. We didn't find patches on her. She could have smoked the drug and so we should probably swab her nose, throat, and trachea. Dr. Baker, have you had a drug overdose like her on your table before?"

"No. In every case I can think of, we found needle marks or pills in the stomach. I haven't had anyone die by transdermal patch. People who smoked it and died were obvious addicts by the degradation of the skin and organs. As you said, she has no signs of physical pain or recent surgery. So perhaps this will turn into a homicide in time. It's an interesting case and that seems to be your area of expertise—strange deaths."

Laura Locklear was stitched closed and Jill was ready to remove her bunny suit when Detective Parnell returned to the suite.

"The husband said that Laura took no medication—she was in good health. She attended a few exercise classes each week. He's shocked that she is dead and that we found fentanyl in her blood. We're still questioning him, but he has an alibi for the approximate time of her death, which we'll follow up on. Dr. Baker, you'll give me any information as test results come in?" he asked, passing her his business card.

"Of course, Detective. We should have some test results tomorrow and others will take a few weeks."

He nodded and he and Jill disposed of their bunny suits and left for his car. An hour later, he dropped her off at her hotel with a lecture about sharing information with him and word that he would stop by in the morning. She and Nathan had planned some group activities for their guests including a golf reservation and a river float trip. She thought she could work the case around those activities. Mostly she was happy to be heading to bed after a long, exciting day. She owed Nathan a wedding night in the future as this day was ending without a drop of romance in her soul at the moment.

She entered the room to find her board filled with new information and her friends still working. Everyone looked tired as it was approaching midnight.

"So what killed her?" Marie asked, looking up from her computer.

"Fentanyl overdose. She hasn't been ruled either an accidental death or a homicide yet."

Everyone paused in their work wondering if they had a case to work on.

"Why would she be a homicide if she died from a drug overdose?" Nathan asked.

"We found fentanyl in her blood, but not her urine. That means the only dose she had was a fatal dose. We found no drug in her stomach or any track marks. So, either Dr. Baker and I missed the track marks, or she used a patch, or she smoked it. So then the next question is—was she a chronic user? Well, she had no surgical scars and in the times that Nathan and I met with her and throughout our ceremony, she didn't act like someone in pain or someone needing a fix of something. She has a healthy liver, so if she's been using, she hasn't been using long. Here's the next problem—if she wanted to apply a patch or smoke fentanyl, why would she walk into the vineyard to do that? Why wouldn't she get in her car and go home? If she was applying a patch, she could have done it in her car or in our porta-potties. If she was smoking it, then I get that she might want to step away from the crowd so no one sees her light up. So instead of having a smoke in her car, she decided to do so in the vineyard. Right?"

Everyone listening nodded that they were following her explanation.

"Okay, then, you apply the patch or patches or inhale or smoke it, and it turns out to be a lethal dose. Right?"

Again, everyone nodded their head.

"I've never been prescribed a fentanyl patch and certainly I'd never smoke anything, let alone an opioid," Angela said, and again the remainder of the room nodded in agreement with her.

"So we find you lying in the vineyard after you've fallen asleep from the opioid. What are we missing?"

"Was she wearing a patch?" Nathan asked, trying to remember the woman where she was slumped in the vineyard.

"No she wasn't. There was no evidence anywhere of a patch—not on her body, not in her purse, there was no wrapper for the patch, nothing lying in the dirt anywhere near her."

"Any matches or a lighter?" Jo asked.

"Again, none on her or nearby, nor was there any kind of flat surface near her that might have contained the fentanyl for snorting or smoking," Jill said.

"How very odd. At least she has you on her case. What are your next steps?" Henrik asked.

Jill smiled at Henrik and said, "Yeah, I don't like mysteries like this. The next steps of the police are to get more test results back, do another search of the church ruin and vineyard, and interview friends and family. She's married with no children, but her husband was away in Nashville with a verified alibi at the time of her death. He said she took no prescription drugs."

"My plane will be leaving in two hours. I must get back to

Germany for work, but contact me if you need my assistance. I have to head out and pack. As usual, you managed to make your wedding ceremony unique and, despite the dead woman, I enjoyed myself. Perhaps I can lead a toast to the newlyweds?"

Everyone held out their glass of wine, tea, or water and toasted Jill and Nathan before taking Henrik's lead and heading for their own suites for the night.

CHAPTER 6

Soon Nathan and Jill were alone and their suite was quiet. "Trust me to give you the strangest wedding night on record," Jill said, sighing with her eyes closed as she was suddenly exhausted.

"As it is after midnight, it's no longer our wedding night. You've got a tough day ahead of you tomorrow as I presume you're going to try and solve the case while golfing and river rafting. Let's head to bed and we'll do a do-over of our wedding night once we return home."

"That sounds like a splendid idea, darling. I really do love you," Jill was sound asleep within minutes of entering their bedroom.

The next morning, she was dressed for their scheduled adventures, ordered room service, and started reviewing her temporary murder board on the living room wall. Nathan was not a morning person and would likely be asleep for a couple of more hours. Her phone rang with twin sounds indicating arriving texts. Marie was also a morning person and was inquiring if Jill was awake, as was Detective Parnell. Jill invited both to join her at the hotel suite. Marie arrived within a minute, while the detective needed twenty minutes to travel.

"I felt bad texting you early after your wedding night, but I know you're always an early riser no matter how late you go to sleep."

"Yeah, I fell asleep soon after entering the bedroom. Nathan and I decided to hold a do-over of our wedding night after we return to California. Detective Parnell is on his way here. Would you like some coffee? I ordered room service anticipating that I would be feeding people until we leave for our tee time."

"Nathan's a wise man. I'll take coffee and food when it arrives."

"I left a voicemail for everyone else who has an interest in this case, to join us when and if they want. I don't have any new information overnight. I'm hoping the detective will have more results from the autopsy and the interviews. They should be doing another search of the vineyard later today looking for transdermal patches or matches."

"So you're planning on playing golf and doing the river float thing today?"

"Yeah, the autopsy is already done, so there's nothing I need to be onsite for, and I can search stuff from anywhere with my phone. Nathan and I aren't golfing; we're just planning on moving from group to group to chat. Did you finish searching all the catering people, the vineyard owners, and the local Presbyterian church?"

"The catering staff, yes. I'll start looking at the vineyard owners, and I believe that Jo is working on the church as she was talking about their finances," Marie said, as she curled up with her laptop and a cup of coffee that she had brought from her room.

Jill nodded and answered the door for room service. They brought in bakery rolls, yogurt, and fresh fruit. Jill debated ordering healthier options like oatmeal and eggs, but she needed the food to be available for three hours and eggs would be gross if they sat that long atop a burner.

The detective arrived as the hotel caterer was leaving with his cart.

"Good morning, Detective. Help yourself to coffee, tea, water, and food if you want. I'm going to grab something."

Jill was silent as she filled her plate and poured her coffee. She set her plate on a coffee table and looked up at her murder board. Once the detective sat down, she started peppering him with questions.

"What did you learn during the interviews? Any new results from the post-mortem? Have you been to the vineyard to search for more evidence yet?"

"I wondered if you would be awake yet given your special day yesterday, but I can see I should have boosted with some caffeine before I arrived. Yes, to all three of your questions," the detective said, pausing to take a bite out of a cheese danish.

Jill waited impatiently. As the hostess she couldn't very well say, "Hurry up and eat," but the glare in her eyes said it for her.

The detective must have noticed and correctly read her glare as he put down his danish, took a sip of coffee, and said, "We searched the vineyard and church ruin and found no evidence of fentanyl packaging. There were no wrappers from a patch or implements to smoke anywhere. The only place we didn't look was the porta-potties as that would be like looking for a needle in a haystack."

Both Marie and Jill wrinkled their nose at that thought, but they had to agree with the detective's statement—it would be very hard to separate the toilet paper and other things in a porta-potty to find evidence.

"That lack of evidence sways my opinion toward you, Dr. Quint, that Laura Locklear may eventually be labeled as a homicide. In my twenty years as a cop, I've never come across an overdose or death by illicit drugs where the paraphernalia of those drugs wasn't nearby."

"Exactly. I've never autopsied someone who took an overdose of a drug, neatly discarded all the trappings of that overdose, and then lay down to die."

"We received more test results from the post-mortem, and there's no evidence according to Dr. Baker that our victim was a chronic user of fentanyl. We were able to interview her physician today and she had no complaints of pain. He had never so much as prescribed any pain relievers for her—no strains or sprains, as he said. He concluded that she was in good health."

"That's the information I expected to gain today," Jill said, giving the detective a look that said continue telling me your findings.

"Let me play Devil's Advocate," Marie said. "Why would someone stand in a vineyard and let someone place a fentanyl patch on her or try and make her inhale smoke of any kind, let alone fentanyl? I wouldn't do either of those things. I'd run, or punch, kick, or slap away at anyone trying to get me to inhale so much as a cigarette."

"So we're looking at means, motive, and opportunity. At the moment, you're having problems with the opportunity piece," Jill said.

Detective Parnell was flooded with feelings about the case. He felt like he was in a weird dream where this woman took over his case. On the other hand, he was learning stuff from her and her team. He'd never seen civilians be so helpful, yet not care what he thought of their efforts. He was like an invisible detective.

"So let's talk about who should be on our list of suspects— everyone who was at the wedding, the vineyard owners, and someone unknown who visited the property to confront Laura. Detective, do you know if there are any cameras on the road leading to that vineyard? I don't know this area well enough to know if there are multiple roads that reach the winery and what is on the road beyond it that would attract car traffic."

Detective Parnell decided he needed to create some separation between his work and that of Dr. Quint. He stood up and said, "I've got to chase more leads, but yes, everyone in the wedding party is a suspect as well as the others you named. There are two ways to get to the vineyard—one coming from town and the other from the next town over. I don't know if any private citizens have cameras along that road. We don't have any city-owned cameras in this region."

He was gone shortly after he finished the last sentence. Jill looked at Marie and asked, "What? You didn't like the bakery or coffee I provided you, Detective Parnell?" And both women laughed remembering other detectives they had irritated over the years.

"What is it about you, Jill, that has any detective running as far as they can to get away from you? Do you exude some pheromone that says, 'run away from Jill Quint?'"

"It was like he suddenly realized he was consulting civilians and had to get away from us as soon as possible. Oh well, it's his loss. At least he's viewing Laura's death as a potential homicide. I think the medical examiner will have to label her death as 'undetermined' because she doesn't have enough facts to view it any other way. Solid detective work will give her cause to change the mode of death to homicide."

"So what are our next steps?" Marie asked.

Jill looked at her watch to judge when everyone would wake up and when they would need to meet for their golf game. She calculated that they had between two and three hours. "I'd like to drive out to the winery and see if we can find any cameras at private residences aimed at the road."

"That might be a little creepy to knock on strangers' doors and ask them if they have video feed from yesterday."

"True. What story can we use? How about if we stick close to the truth? I have my business cards that say I am a forensic pathologist and private detective. They won't think to ask me who hired me, and of course, the answer is I hired myself as it was my wedding."

"It's a flimsy answer, but let's see if we can run with it. I'll grab my purse and jacket and meet you back here. We should leave a note as Nathan won't be awake for hours, and your mother and Nathan's parents won't know who to ask about what's going on."

"Good point. I'll take care of that communication now."

Jill wrote text messages and left voicemails for everyone concerned, and Marie returned with Angela in tow.

"Hey! Good morning. Are you going to join us?"

"Yeah. Let me grab some water and fruit and we can go. I've got my camera, so I'm ready to record our morning," she said patting the camera case strung across her body.

Fifteen minutes later, they were on the road to the vineyard after traveling through the town of Asheville. Jill drove slowly, pulling over to let cars pass on the surprisingly busy road.

"There's a car about every five minutes on this road. It's busier than I thought it would be," Jill said.

"You're driving slow, but it's still hard to search for cameras. Perhaps we need to only slow down when we see a private gate abutting the road. That's probably where we'll see a camera that might have a view of the road," Angela suggested.

"Yeah, I think you're right about that," Marie agreed.

Jill sped up her driving and they finally saw a gate protecting a house somewhere behind it. The leaves were changing on some trees in preparation for the coming winter. They had seen better leaf displays, but this one wasn't bad.

Jill pulled to the side of the road and the three of them walked back to the gate looking for a camera. Marie pointed at two cameras one in front of the gate and one that was likely for identifying anyone seeking entry to the house. Jill pressed the buzzer on the pin pad and waited for a response. There was none. She pressed the button again and still there was no response.

"I wonder if they think we're salespeople of some type?" Marie said.

"Or maybe we're church missionaries," Angela suggested.

"Or maybe no one is home," Jill said. "Let's write the address down and perhaps our fearless Detective Parnell can follow up. Let's continue along the road and see if we can find another gate like this where someone answers our doorbell."

They drove for another mile or so before coming upon another gate. This time Jill parked her rental car in front of the gate while they searched for cameras that might be aimed at the road. They found a camera, but it was aimed more at the driver's side of the car and angled toward the hood rather than toward the trunk and the road behind it, so they continued their search.

Jill was afraid she was going to run out of the road as they were approaching the vineyard and still they hadn't found the relevant street cameras. She continued and sure enough, they came upon the little parking lot next to the church ruin. The porta-potties had been removed, but otherwise, it looked the same as yesterday. Jill smiled at the church and pulled into the lot.

"Let's take a look here just in case the crime scene folks missed something. It was dusk yesterday and foggy this morning, so maybe they didn't see a piece of evidence that they might have found in the bright sunlight."

They started by searching the parking lot.

"What am I'm looking for?" Angela asked. "It's not every day that I'm looking for evidence of fentanyl."

Jill smiled and said, "Good point. The patches come in a square package, sort of what you see with condom packing—a foil background with clear plastic covering the patch. You pull the patch out and peel off the plastic covering the drug side of the patch and place it on your skin. If she smoked the fentanyl, then we need a lighter, matches, foil, or a spoon as people heat it up. We should also search the grounds looking for disturbed soil in case evidence was buried in the dirt."

"Okay, this might be the strangest stuff I've ever looked for," Angela said, as the three of them started looking for clues.

They spent about forty-five minutes searching for evidence in the church ruin, the parking lot, and the vineyard. All three came up with no new evidence. As they stood by the car, Jill suggested that they look up and down the road perhaps one hundred yards. If Laura Locklear was murdered, then her killer could have parked somewhere besides the parking lot for the church ruin and discarded materials there.

Marie and Jill took one side of the road while Angela took the other. They met back at the car again and as Angela approached, she held a paper bag toward Jill.

"Here you go."

"Whatcha got?" asked Marie.

"Maybe something, maybe nothing. I found a piece of cellophane down the road, and I wondered if it might be connected to the fentanyl patch that you mentioned."

Jill opened the bag the paper bag and looked in and said, "This could be the wrapper for a fentanyl patch. I'll ask the detective to send it to the lab to see if it's positive for fentanyl. Do you remember where you picked it up?"

Angela said, "Here's a picture. You know me, I always take pictures when we work on these cases."

"You're the best," Jill said. "I'm going to give the detective a call to see if he can analyze the cellophane for the presence of fentanyl."

"Have you heard back from the autopsy yet as to whether they found fentanyl in her throat or nose? Wouldn't that be the proof you need that she smoked it?" Marie asked.

"Yes, that would be proof and I haven't heard back so I'll ask the detective about that," Jill said. "I'm still bothered as to why she would willingly let someone place a patch on her or make her smoke a fentanyl cigarette or however she inhaled it. I'm sitting on the fence as to whether this is an accidental case or homicide."

Jill leaned against the car and called the detective. She got his voicemail and left him a message about the evidence they collected. She let him know that she would drop it off at the police station on her way back to the hotel.

"Do you think we should continue down the road in the opposite direction from Asheville and see if any of the homes have cameras on the road? If she was killed, it doesn't necessarily mean that the killer came from the direction of Asheville," Marie said.

"That's a good suggestion. Let's go," Jill said, as they all stepped into the car.

They came across one house with cameras on the road. Again, they tried to gain an entrance or otherwise talk to the occupant, but they got no response. Jill noted the address to pass on to the detective.

It was time to return to their hotel and get ready for first the golf game, and then the river raft excursion for the friends and family who had attended their wedding. It was time to set murder aside and enjoy the love and companionship of friends and family.

CHAPTER 7

 ost of the friends and family had signed up for
the golf game. They decided in advance to play a
scramble. That way, Jill and Nathan could rotate among the
groups golfing and spend a little time with each guest. Each
team of golfers had something positive to say about the
wedding, and then immediately wanted to know what the latest
news was and whether Jill had found the person who killed her
officiant.

By the fourth group of golfers, Jill said to Nathan as they
walked, "I'm glad everyone enjoyed our wedding, but I feel like a
broken record. Talking about what we're looking for in terms of
determining if Laura was murdered or died accidentally. Can
you think of anything else to talk about?"

"I wouldn't even try. There's a reason people love murder-
mystery dinners and mystery train rides and escape rooms.
People love puzzles, including your friends. Maybe you'll luck
out and one of them will have a suggestion of a fresh look that
you could take with this case."

When Jill and Nathan joined the group containing her

mother, Barbara asked, "Did you find anything besides the fentanyl in her blood? I think I saw that on a TV show once."

"You know, Mom, that's not a bad idea. I just heard the result about the fentanyl in blood and urine, and I didn't look any further. But she could have been knocked out by something else. Maybe I can get the results of the blood work from the coroner in Charlotte. Thanks for that suggestion."

Jill's mother seemed flustered by the fact that she might have suggested a new angle for her daughter to take in solving this crime. They both hugged her and moved on to the next group.

As they were between the two groups, Jill cell phone rang with Detective Parnell's number.

"Hello, Detective."

"Dr. Quint, I have new information for you, and I've been advised to use your expertise as much as possible."

"My team and I are only trying to help, and we're not amateurs. I've worked on over one thousand autopsies and my team has assisted on twenty to thirty murder cases worldwide."

"Yeah, well, the cellophane did have fentanyl on it as well as a fingerprint. Here's our problem: The fingerprint has not come up with a match, and we don't know if it has anything to do with this crime. Someone could've thrown it out the window as they were driving along that road."

"True. However, I don't like coincidences, and this appears to be one of those. I wanted to get a second look at all the blood work the coroner, Dr. Baker, ordered in Charlotte. I'd also like to swab Laura's face to see if there's any residue on it. Is there a chance you could give me access to results and request that additional testing be done? I'd be happy to sign a confidentiality agreement."

"To be honest, I've never worked with someone like you before, but a confidentiality agreement sounds like a good thing. Let me have our county counsel design some kind of confidentiality statement. Hopefully, by the time I call you back, I'll have both lab results and that agreement for you."

"Thank you, Detective. I really do want to help. Nathan and I liked Laura Locklear and chose her to be our officiant at our wedding. Given my occupation, I owe her my time to determine if she is an accidental overdose or a homicide."

"I thought you were convinced she was a homicide?"

"I'm stuck on why Laura would let someone put a patch on her or force her to smoke fentanyl, but if she did it on purpose, then why didn't we find any fentanyl evidence around her? That is why I need further test results. We're missing a big piece of the puzzle. Fentanyl can kill within two minutes. Unless she dug a hole somewhere in that vineyard, took the drug, then buried the evidence and lay down to die, this must be a homicide. We searched the church and the vineyard for soil disruptions but didn't see any."

"I'm not sure my team looked for soil disruptions. I'll ask them that question. Let me get any additional test results from the M.E.'s office and I'll forward them to you. Hopefully, they'll present you with another clue."

"Hopefully. Thank you, Detective."

They ended the call, and Jill and Nathan resumed their stroll toward the next group.

"He seems cooperative. That's a refreshing change," Nathan said, having heard Jill's side of the conversation.

"He does. I don't know if it is because he checked my references, or if he is as puzzled as I am about this case."

"Given the interactions over the years that I've watched you have with other police agencies, I think it's likely that he checked your references, and someone told him to get your services for free."

"Aren't you a cynic? Though you're right that this won't pad our vacation account. However, how could I not try and solve Laura's murder? I thought she did a great job at our wedding.

She made it memorable and meaningful, and I'm not sure what she could have done to make it better than it was."

"You offer me such romantic thoughts at the oddest time," Nathan said with a smile as he stopped to hug and kiss Jill.

"Hey, you two newlyweds, no making out on the golf course," they heard Nathan's brother, Matthew, shout. "You might get hit by a golf ball."

They broke apart, rueful at being caught in a private moment, and approached the next golf team.

Once they were within talking range, Matthew added, "Though to be fair, you've had your honeymoon interrupted by murder."

"Actually, I had to kiss Jill when she told me how wonderful our wedding was and that was part of the reason she was pursuing the cause of our officiant's death. That's a really romantic statement, coming from Jill."

Jill gave him an elbow to his side and said, "I can't be that bad in the romance department or you wouldn't have proposed marriage."

"That's true," he said, reaching an arm around her waist.

"Any news on the murder?" asked his mother, Brenda.

Jill went through her usual explanation and gave them the update from her recent call.

"You were out searching for evidence this morning?" Nathan's father, Charles, asked.

"Yeah, I'm a morning lark while Nathan is a morning zombie. I always work my cases in the early morning, especially since a few of my team members are larks also. We searched the wedding venue and the road leading to it earlier this morning. We were looking for homes that had cameras trained on the road in hopes of being able to analyze the vehicles coming and going."

"That's a rather gruesome thing to be doing that day after

your wedding. Nathan, why weren't you up helping her?" Brenda asked.

"Mom, Jill and I dated for three years before our wedding yesterday. My role in her cases is to cook and hydrate her and her team. Perhaps on every fifth or so case I suggest something that spurs her team on, or I end up defending her from the suspect. Jill's correct that I'm a zombie in the morning and my being there wouldn't have helped her case. I know it's been a long time since I lived at your house, but was there ever a time when I was a morning lark?"

"No, we should have remembered. What if the suspect attacked her?" Charles asked.

"No one knows she's working on this case except Detective Parnell and the medical examiner, Dr. Baker, so I don't have any worries for her safety yet. If she or her team interviews any of the suspects, then I'll need to start worrying as that may alert the suspect that Jill is on to them."

"Many of my friends have been married in the past five years, and I have to say this is the weirdest wedding conversation that I've ever heard," Matthew said. "I'm thinking that future wedding receptions will be dull compared to yours, Nathan."

"We aim to provide unique experiences. We could talk wine if that will make you feel better," Jill said, smiling.

"Gosh, no. The conversation will go from weird to boring. My brother is the wine expert and I only rarely tap into his wine knowledge if I'm buying a special gift; otherwise, I tune out all wine words."

They all laughed and talked a little about golf and the setting, and then the couple moved on to the next group. It contained a random collection of Jill's friends and Nathan's employee, Joshua. Alicia was a Forensic Pathologist in New Orleans, and Melissa was a fellow vintner from Jill's area. In a prior life, Melissa was a criminal psychologist. Jill knew this would be a longer conversation as the three of them had missed the discussion last night. Both Melissa and Alicia had made evening plans with friends.

Jill gave them all the facts while Nathan chatted with his employee, who had assisted with the decorations and would be working on wine labels that Nathan was designing for local wineries.

Melissa asked, "Based on what you described so far and the behavior that I observed at your ceremony, I would agree that your officiant's death is very suspicious. She didn't behave like addicts I've met over the years or as someone on the verge of suicide. Would you like me to join your group tonight?"

"If you have time. It would be great for you to meet the members of my team. There's no pay involved in this case; I'm involved out of respect and appreciation for our officiant."

"No problem, I'll do what I can. What time tonight?"

"How about seven? We are river floating after this golf game and then we have a taco bar planned for anyone who wants to join us. As soon as everyone is done eating and leaves, we'll go to work on whatever new information has been generated today and our strategy for tomorrow."

"You're such a wonderful host," Nathan said. "I suspect almost no one is going to leave. Everyone wants to help you. Better still, you don't have any gross pictures to ruin anyone's digestion."

"My friends should be used to our weird conversations. We'll have some newbies and maybe they'll have some new ideas. We have one more group to meet and pretty much everyone will be up to speed. I should have new data from the detective later today, and I'll invite him to join us, but I can't imagine he'll say yes. See you guys later."

Nathan and Jill reached the final group and conducted nearly the same conversation as they had with all the previous groups. They wished the group well and were headed back to their hotel suite to make sure all the preparations were moving forward.

Jill sat down on the sofa with a sigh, "I'm tired of telling the same story what—ten, twelve times?"

"There were ten groups, and they are enjoying themselves. I think we made a good decision to stop by each group rather than play ourselves."

"Yeah, I think that was a good choice too."

"So far, except for the death of our officiant, this wedding has been pretty perfect. Do you think you'll have an answer about Laura's death before we return to California?"

"I hope so. Everyone's leaving tomorrow, but depending on their day jobs, we'll still get work done. I'm hoping to get some more results from the autopsy that will help direct our attention. Also, I don't have much of a motive yet. I need to talk more with Marie and Jo to see what they found out about Laura. Of course, I want to check the alibi of the husband once again as he should be top of anyone's list."

"Little did I know that when I arranged for a casual taco bar dinner, it would turn into a murder mystery dinner. Unlike those fictional dinners, someone is already dead, and no one will die from tacos."

Jill leaned into kiss Nathan. "You really are the best. Not only do you go with the flow, but you keep us well fed while you're going with that flow."

"My life is certainly never boring around you. Your cases have brought interesting people into our lives. I really enjoy Henrik's friendship and I wish our dear departed friend Nick could've been at the wedding. I also have probably expanded my business because of the cases you've gotten involved with, so I have no complaints."

They enjoyed the afternoon filled with laughter and conversation as they floated down the French Broad River. Jill and Nathan received compliments about their organization of wedding activities. No one had to have skill at golf or river rafting to enjoy what the day had been filled with. Still, Jill could sense everyone's anticipation of the conversation that night. She hoped someone would have a new angle that she and her team hadn't thought of yet. She'd invited the detective to join them, but he declined. He had supplied her with additional information that gave her some ideas and solidified her thoughts about homicide versus an accidental death.

CHAPTER 8

Jill was eating her last taco and noticed that the volume of discussion was decreasing. It was like her friends and family wanted her to finish eating quickly so they could move on and help her solve the murder. She smiled inwardly and slowed her chewing to make this last taco take even longer than the first two had.

Nathan leaned over and whispered, "Sweetheart, I know you're enjoying torturing your friends and family by eating slowly, but everyone's level of anticipation is giving me indigestion. Would you hurry up and finish that taco!?"

Jill gave Nathan a brilliant smile and did as he asked. In under a minute, she was using a napkin to make sure she had no food remaining on her face. She took a sip of her margarita and moved to where she had borrowed a large dry-erase board earlier and had written details on it. She flipped it over to dead silence in the room.

"I have new information that the detective gave me after we returned from our boat float. Many of you may not understand what some of this data means, so I'll explain that and then we'll move on to theories as to why Laura was murdered."

"That's interesting. You've now concluded that she was murdered," Marie said. "What changed your mind?"

"The analysis of her clothing came back. She was gassed with fentanyl. It's homicide. It can't be suicide as the source of the gas wasn't left near her body, likewise, the same explanation for accidental death."

"Where does someone buy fentanyl gas? Do you have to be a dentist or doctor to get it?" Jo asked.

"I don't know as I haven't tried to acquire it. I would think you would need a medical license for a prescription. This may be a synthetic fentanyl gas made in any illegal lab. It will take a little more analysis to determine that. The Russian military also used fentanyl gas to stop fifty well-armed Chechen rebels who took more than eight hundred people hostage in a theater in 2002. They accidentally killed over a hundred theatergoers, so it wasn't a great hostage strategy."

"I might be able to help with those questions," Barbara said. "Back in my working days, I was a chemist. I'll take charge of collecting options on where to obtain fentanyl gas—legal or otherwise."

"Thanks, Mom. Somehow, I forgot what you did in your life before kids," Jill said, smiling ruefully. "I guess it's time to start compiling a list of our suspects. We have a time of death within about forty-five minutes. Angela, why don't you document as many of us in the wedding reception to coincide with the time of death? If anyone else has pictures taken between two and three, send them to Angela. It would be nice to eliminate everyone in this room."

"Are you saying we're suspects?" Nathan's mother asked. Her expression said she didn't know whether to be appalled or thrilled at being on the list.

"Yes, all of us are suspects as we could have stepped outside and quickly put Laura Locklear to sleep permanently out in the vineyard," Jill replied. "Have a gas canister in our purse, walk up to her with a question about the local area that requires Laura to step into the vineyard, then you gas her. At least that is what I would think if I was the police."

"Well, I'll verify that my husband and sons were inside between two and three."

"That's nice, but it's not a witness statement that would hold up as you have an interest in declaring your immediate family innocent. We need proof."

"Oh, my."

"Next, we need to work on a motive. Nathan and I liked Laura from the moment we met her. Though we come from different religious backgrounds, she did an excellent job adapting the ceremony to our needs. She seemed to have respect within the local Presbyterian church, and taught a class to kids. She also had her officiant license as she had married someone else. She's been married a decade to a man, and they have no children. I don't know much about her husband, parents, siblings, friends. Her husband, according to the police, has a verified alibi of being in Nashville which is a four-hour drive from here. I don't know everything about her role in the church. I think we can safely say that this isn't a random murder by a stranger. Our suspect did significant research to develop a plan to kill Laura for reasons unknown. Somewhere out there in the universe is a person with a reason to kill Laura Locklear."

"Do you know if the suspect is male or female?" Nathan's father asked.

"I don't. It could be either. In fact, it could be a teenager. I'd say it could be a child except there is some sophistication in acquiring the fentanyl gas that we wouldn't expect to find in a child. Mom, we might be able to narrow our suspects if we could figure out the cost of acquiring fentanyl gas."

"On it," her mother replied looking up from where she was doing research on her laptop. Jill gave a brief thought to her mother's enthusiasm for solving the mystery around Laura

Locklear's death and made a checkmark in her mind to include her mom in the future if she had questions about chemistry. Jill took chemistry during her education, and she understood the medical processes of chemistry, but she had no knowledge of the industrial side of where one obtained products. Jill was glad to see that her mom was enjoying being a researcher.

"As I mentioned earlier when we were in a smaller group, the local Presbyterian church has had financial problems recently. They benefited during the pandemic with a loan from the government for small business that doesn't have to be paid back. I'll do some more research into that and determine if our victim played any role in the financial business of the church," Jo said.

"As the Queen of social media analysis, I could use some help to do a deeper dive into all the suspects involved in this case. Does anyone else in the room have that skill set?" Marie asked looking at Nathan's brother.

"I'm a computer geek; if you show me your process, I can follow it and start searching," Matthew Conroy said.

"As some of you know, in a prior life I was a forensic psychologist. So I'll join Marie and give a brief opinion on each suspect in regards to criminal behavior," Melissa offered. "There's no science behind my opinion; rather, it will be based on my years of experience of predicting who will become a criminal."

"I'd like to interview the people at the church whom Laura worked with to see if I can get anything out of them," Angela said. "Anyone want to come with me?"

"I will since I have a PI license, and therefore our questioning becomes more legitimate," Jill said.

Jill's new mother-in-law indicated she would tag along.

"It looks like everyone has their assignments. I think I'll take a leaf out of my son's playbook and stay here. I'll help Nathan with keeping you all fed and hydrated. Hopefully, also like my son, I'll have that occasional brilliant question that helps you solve the case," Charles Conroy said.

"Bring the wine, tea, water, everything else to all the researchers, and we'll get started. Angela, Brenda, and I will work on a list of people and questions that we'll use for interviewing tomorrow. I think it's too late on a Saturday night to knock on the doors of perfect strangers and ask them questions. Also, despite that wonderful taco bar, I'll be ready for dessert in an hour or so and I'll leave that to Nathan's and his father's capable hands."

By the end of the night, Jill and Angela, with input from Brenda, had their schedule planned for the next day. They would start at the caterers and see how many people they could interview at that location who had worked the wedding. Fortunately, the bakery was open on Sunday. Once they were done with the caterers, they planned to move on to a variety of church people. It could be problematic given that they would be asking questions on a Sunday. On the other hand, they might easily find the people they were looking for at church rather than chasing them down in their residences.

Jill had kept her ear open to Marie's group and was glad that she had help given the many people on their list of suspects. They created a master document and were adding information as they discovered it. She spent a few moments on her own reviewing more evidence that was shared with her. The blood chemistry data resulted from someone who had simply stopped breathing. Otherwise, their victim was in excellent health.

She tried to imagine the scene. Had someone convinced Laura to take a walk in the vineyard and then hit her with a surprise fentanyl gas attack, or did the gas attack occur elsewhere and she was dragged to her final resting place? Jill had taken a few pictures of the crime scene after Laura was removed. She didn't see any drag marks in her pictures and couldn't recall any in her mind's picture of the scene. Of course, a strong adult probably could have picked Laura up in a fireman's carry and then dropped her where they found her. It made more sense to her that a person approached Laura as soon as she exited the reception and coaxed their victim to walk into the vineyard.

Work continued throughout the room. There was Jo's loud clacking of the keys, and Marie's group who were working both together and apart. Jill's mother was in a world of her own, chasing the mystery of fentanyl gas. Nathan and his father were making noise in the kitchen, which was surely a sign that dessert was on its way. If Jill recalled correctly, most of the wedding attendees were leaving tomorrow evening. Only Angela was staying over as she would be working with Nathan to collect photographs for a new winery that had hired him. She wondered where the case would be in another twenty-four hours. Jill and Nathan were returning to California on Tuesday. They didn't need to be in the same room to solve this case, but her friends were all returning to their day jobs, which took precedence over this case of their murdered officiant. By the end of the evening when people were flagging, Nathan and his father served a light dessert and they parted ways, planning to resume in the morning. Jill, Angela, and Brenda would begin their interview circuit at an early hour and go from there.

CHAPTER 9

The group learned a lot about Laura as Marie was an early riser and added notes to Jill's dry erase board about their victim. Laura was born into a large farming family elsewhere in North Carolina. She met her husband at college and had a degree in history. She taught middle-grade history at various schools. Her reviews were favorable from kids and parents alike. She also taught in the student ministry. The curriculum seemed a combination of teaching students about God and group activities around sports and crafts.

There seemed to be nothing negative about Laura or her husband, Thomas, anywhere online. Thomas also volunteered in the church. His day job appeared to be that of an accountant, and he was in Nashville for a seminar on upcoming tax changes. He was on Jill's list to interview. He also had a fairly large family, which they would explore during the interview.

Everything that Marie researched about their victim pointed to her being a woman loved by everyone. Still, there was someone out there who hated her enough to kill her because this was not a random act of violence.

Jill wasn't sure how this interview process was going to go

as, though she had spent time with Nathan's mother in the past, she had never seen her in the position of gaining information through interviews. She liked to give Angela the lead and only speak if she thought of something based on what Angela had asked. She'd make sure that Brenda knew to let Angela take the lead. She knew Brenda to be a quiet person, so Jill admitted to herself that she was surprised that her mother-in-law had volunteered for this task.

Before they set out, the three of them decided on the questions they would ask in general. They agreed they would only ask the question "What were you doing at the time of Laura Locklear's death," if something came out in the interview to make them suspicious. Generally, most people didn't appreciate being asked what they were doing at the time of someone's murder. It was better to set a tone of "what did you see?" The whole interview could go sideways as Jill and her team were not the police and people were not required to talk to them.

"Do you have on your list the other couple that Laura officiated for?" Brenda asked.

"I don't, but I should—good idea, Mom. Marie, can you find the other couple's name and address for us?" Jill asked. Marie looked up and nodded, indicating with her look that it would be child's play to find the requested information.

Soon, they were organized with whom they were talking to and in what order, guessing who might be where on what looked to be a lovely Sunday. As they were stopping by the bakery first, they planned to eat breakfast to assuage their own hunger and support the bakery. With Jill's sweet tooth, this wasn't a difficult activity to manage.

Jill arrived at the bakery and noted that the owner with whom she had arranged her wedding reception was behind the counter. She was also grateful to note that the bakery had two customers dining and no one else in line.

"Hello, Rachel, do you have a minute to talk?" Jill asked.

The woman looked concerned and Jill quickly added that she was very happy with the bakery's catering for her wedding.

"I can show you the review I posted two days ago. I don't know if you've heard, but the woman who officiated our ceremony was murdered in the vineyard sometime during the reception. I just wanted to talk to you and your staff to see if any of you saw anything suspicious or out of the ordinary. Have the police been by to interview you and your staff?"

"Oh my gosh! I hadn't heard that. Maybe it hasn't been on the news yet. What was the woman's name again?"

"Laura Locklear."

"Hmm, I don't know that name, so I must not know her personally. Asheville has over three hundred thousand people living here, so I admit to not knowing everyone. I've learned stuff about my regular customers and business owners through the Chamber of Commerce, but that's a small group. Dare I ask how she was murdered?"

Jill paused momentarily to think about how to respond. In the end, she decided she wasn't sharing something that the police weren't sharing. It was likely in the press release announcing the murder because if the cause of death wasn't listed, journalists hounded the media for answers.

"Someone blew fentanyl gas at her face. That caused her to relax, then fall asleep, then stop breathing, and then she died."

"Wow. I guess if you have to get murdered, that's not a bad way to go. Mind you, no one should be killed."

"Yeah, I have to agree with you," Angela said. "By the way, that was a beautiful spread that you provided on such short notice for Jill's wedding. Thanks for having vegetarian options, and the wedding cake was simple but tasty." Rachel smiled at the compliment. Angela continued, "We think Laura died about an hour into the reception. Do you think that you or any of your servers might've noticed anything at that time?"

"Let me think. That was two days ago, and I wasn't paying

particular attention to time. I know I didn't step outside of the church until I was cleaning up around four in the afternoon. Half of my staff had left by then, and my husband, Jeff, was helping me load the van. From what you just said, the woman was already dead and lying in the vineyard at that time. I exited the church door and turned left to walk toward the parking lot, as did my husband. Would we have been able to see Laura lying in the vineyard from that angle?"

"No. You also couldn't see her from the parking lot. Did you notice any cars in the area that were parked along the road that led to the church?" Angela asked.

"No. I was concentrating on not tripping with big pans in my hands. I was also thinking about what went well and what I would do differently for the next event, so I wouldn't have noticed if any cars drove by or even parked by the roadside. I usually get to the bakery at four in the morning to begin baking, so by the time I was cleaning up after your reception it had been a long day."

"Are your husband and the employees who assisted you at the reception available? We'd like to speak with them, too," Angela asked.

"There's an employee in the back who worked the reception and I'll send her out to talk to you. My husband is home with the kids, and the other employees are off today," Rachel said.

"I don't remember seeing a male server at the reception. Did your husband just assist you at the end with cleanup, or was he there earlier?" Angela asked.

"I wasn't sure what time the reception would end, so I called him when I noticed things were winding down. I would guess that was about three and he arrived about twenty minutes later. So, I can't imagine that he would be of much help in answering your questions."

Angela nodded and said, "If you don't mind, we'd love to order breakfast and coffee and chat with your employee if that's possible. It's strictly voluntary on her part, but we would like to have a few minutes of her time."

"I'll ask her and tell her it's voluntary. She's on her break for another ten minutes and I don't want to interrupt that, but I think I can spare her at the counter."

"Thank you," Angela said, and they placed their orders. A few other customers came and went while they ate their breakfast. They noticed that Rachel was pointing a young woman, perhaps in her early twenties, toward them. She had entered the bakery from a swinging door behind which they caught a glimpse of the kitchen.

"Hi, I'm Elizabeth. Rachel said you wanted to talk to me about the wedding reception."

"Yes. I was the bride at the event you catered for me on Friday. Sadly, the woman who officiated my marriage was later found dead in the vineyard that was next to the church. I'm a private investigator from California and I would like to help find whoever killed Laura Locklear."

As Angela was so much more tactful than Jill, she took over the conversation at that point. "Sorry to deliver such distressing news on a Sunday morning, but that's why we wanted to talk with you. What time did you leave the reception on Friday?"

"I'm so sorry to hear of your officiant's death. She was marvelous at performing your wedding ceremony. I left about two hours after the reception started as everyone had had their first serving of lunch and dessert, so there wasn't a need for all of us to stay."

"When you left, did someone pick you up, or was your car out in the parking lot?"

"I drove myself and parked along the road as the parking lot next to the church was filled when I arrived to set up for the reception. So, I returned to my car when I was done working the reception. The parking lot was tiny as they didn't have cars at the time the church was built."

"I hadn't thought about the reason for the size of that parking lot. When you left the church, did you turn left or right to return to the parking lot?" Angela asked.

"I turned left. Are you asking me that to see if I noticed a dead body?"

"No. I'm pretty sure if you had seen a dead body you would've told someone, and she wasn't noticed for about another hour lying on the dirt. I'm just trying to visualize your movements when you finished working. Did you use the bathrooms while you were there?"

"No. I didn't need to. My home is only about twenty minutes from there and truthfully, I'd rather use my home toilet than any porta-potties no matter how elegant they looked."

"I know what you mean," Angela said wrinkling her nose with memories of less savory porta-potties. "I always try to avoid using porta-potties too. Were there any cars parked along the road when you parked or when you left?"

Elizabeth thought for a moment and then said, "I pulled in behind a dark-colored SUV on the side of the road."

"Did it belong to someone you know? Possibly a co-worker?" Elizabeth shook her head "no." Angela then asked, What do you remember about the SUV? For example, was it a big SUV? Did it have North Carolina plates on it? Was there anybody sitting inside of it that you noticed?"

After another pause in which Elizabeth was clearly trying to remember a sliver of time on Friday, she said, "I parked, then exited the car, and hustled over to the church as I was running a few minutes late. I'd say it was a medium-sized SUV and I didn't notice the plates. I might have seen a woman in the front seat as I rushed away. There was definitely someone there and for some reason, I thought they might be putting the final touches of makeup on—lipstick or mascara, as I think they were looking into a mirror above the steering wheel. That's all I remember. Any other questions?"

Angela gave Brenda and Jill a quick look and neither had further questions, so she said, "Elizabeth, thank you so much for your time. Also, thank you for the service you provided at the reception. We loved it and Jill has left positive reviews everywhere she could about how wonderful the bakery was with the last-minute wedding."

The woman nodded and returned to her space behind the counter saying something to her boss. Jill, Angela, and Brenda cleaned up the table they were sitting at and disposed of the paper products their breakfast had been served on. They waved and exited the bakery.

CHAPTER 10

"The breakfast was lovely and the bakery staff congenial, but did we learn anything new?" Brenda asked.

"We did learn a few things. People who left the reception had a tendency to go left to reach the parking lot, rather than right where they might've seen our victim lying on the soil. The human brain tells you to go left as it's shorter than going right. Also, if you're right-handed you have an intuitive bias to turn right. Did either of you notice anyone who arrived late to the wedding?"

"I think because we were all from out of this area and didn't know where the church was, all of us arrived early. There was no door into the church ruin so we couldn't hear anyone arrive late. That's a good question for everybody else who attended—did they notice any late arrivals?" Angela said.

"Yes, that's an excellent question. I'll go over the guest list, but I can only think of a few women who would have arrived by themselves. The woman could've pulled over to take a cell phone call or to search for something in her car and then got caught up freshening her makeup. Also, given how the murderer killed our victim, we know it didn't take great physical strength and therefore could be anyone sophisticated enough to find fentanyl gas."

Brenda clasped Jill's hand and said, "Jill, I'm really enjoying working with you on this mystery. I like the officiant that you and Nathan chose, and I want to help find her murderer. We were supposed to leave today, but I'm going to have Charles extend our stay until you and Nathan return to California. I want to help," Brenda said.

Jill didn't know what to think of Brenda's offer. As far she was concerned, the older woman hadn't contributed yet to the case. On the other hand, usually the more brains the better. Also, most importantly, it would be a small effort on Jill's part to win Nathan's mom's approval, which was something that wouldn't hurt in a new marriage. That was probably a good thing if she ever understood the danger that Jill's cases caused Nathan. She had flashbacks of the knife-wielding guy in Belgium, the Russian mob in Québec, and the cave that they hid in from the mafia in Sicily. It was a good decision to accept Brenda's help.

"I'd appreciate your help. Thank you."

Angela smiled at Jill, silently conveying her approval at her response to Brenda's question. She added, "Jill needs some help. I think nearly everyone else is leaving later today to return to their day jobs. Most of us help Jill from a distance, but in the case of interviewing people, you need to do it face-to-face to be the most effective. Although I am staying, Nathan and I will be out doing a photography shoot tomorrow, though our first appointment isn't until noon. I can help in the morning. So, it will be just the two of you trying to gain information out of people tomorrow."

"That's true, Angela. It doesn't give us much time to solve this case before we all leave the area. At this point, I don't have any obvious suspect," Jill said. "So, I feel we're still at the beginning of this case. At least we identified the murder weapon. That would've been really strange if we couldn't do that."

"Obviously, on TV they solve murders in forty-five minutes. This is a lot more complicated. It's interesting to see what happens when someone dies with no witnesses nearby," Brenda said.

"Actually, there was a witness. It was the murderer. We just have to find out who he or she is and what their motive for the murder was, as that will help convict them."

"What's next on our list?" Brenda asked.

"We're heading to the Presbyterian church where Nathan and I originally met with Laura. They have two hours between church services on Sunday. So I'm timing our arrival to coincide, I hope, with the end of the first service. I think we're going to have to spread out and individually question people; otherwise we'll lose them. Brenda, do you feel comfortable questioning people at the church?"

"I'll write out a list of questions for you, Brenda. If anyone asks why you're asking, just tell them you work for Jill's private detective company," Angela said.

"What's the name of the company in case they ask?"

"I don't have a company name because I don't have a company, but if they ask, say it's *Quint Investigations*. If need be, I can give you my business cards with my name and occupation on them."

"I thought you had a name for your consulting service?" Angela asked.

"No, I have a website that says "Call me if you want a second opinion on the cause of death," and that's been working for at least five years. I didn't get my PI license until at least three years ago, and if you look me up, I don't mention it on my website. Maybe when I get back home, I'll come up with a name and upgrade my website to include investigative services as well as autopsies. My problem is I only want private investigations related to the murder case that I'm working on. I don't want anybody calling me to trail somebody for a divorce case, so I guess that's why I haven't bothered updating my website."

"We have about all the work we can handle given our day jobs. I have to agree with you that you don't want to add that service and advertise it publicly," Angela said.

Jill had timed their arrival perfectly, as people were exiting as though the service had just finished.

"I'm going to seek out the church administrative people. This is Laura's church, and given what we learned about her through our investigations, I'm sure she was well-known. I can't imagine that her husband will be here today, but maybe we can find other people who were Laura's friends or knew her well. See what you can learn by working the crowd."

"Has her death been announced? I didn't read the local paper. The bakery staff didn't know that she was dead. We'll do poorly if we walk up to strangers and ask about her in the past tense," Angela said.

"Good point. Let me look on the phone and see if it was announced in the local paper or on the news stations," Jill said. All three of them used their phones to search for news about Laura Locklear.

"It's on the front page of the local newspaper. Still, not everyone will have read the paper or have heard about her death," Jill said.

"If she was a regular member of this congregation, I would expect the minister to announce her death and ask that Laura be kept in their prayers," Angela said.

Brenda looked uncomfortable knowing that she was heading into likely tough conversations with perfect strangers. Then she shrugged her shoulders and thought, "I don't know anyone here and hopefully I won't offend anyone."

Jill headed into the church to where she knew the administrative offices to be. Brenda and Angela wished each other good luck and moved to tackle the parishioners, targeting women about the age of Laura Locklear. It seemed as though everyone knew her, and they were flooded with questions and stories about her.

An hour later, the three of them met back at the car to discuss their findings.

Jill went first. "People in the administrative office were teary-eyed when I brought up Laura's death. I do think this is a good sign indicating she was held in high regard. I probed for someone who was unhappy with her, but the office couldn't give me any names. The husband is also highly thought of in the church and is holding her memorial service here in a few days. Other than that, I didn't get anything valuable from my interview."

"I spoke with three different women who I guessed to be in Laura's age range." Brenda said. "I'll admit I was shy about breaking into conversations. Like you found, Jill, no one would say anything bad about her. Maybe Angela had better luck."

"I did have a little more luck than you two. I managed to find a woman who considered Laura Locklear her best friend."

"Score!" Jill exclaimed, giving Angela a fist bump.

"The woman's name is Jennifer Bennett and their friendship has lasted over ten years. She said Laura was a devout woman of God, always optimistic, and overall just a wonderful friend. I asked her if she could recall Laura telling her about anyone who was upset with her or if anyone had been unpleasant to Laura recently."

"And?" Jill asked.

"She said that Laura was worried about the church finances. She tried talking to the executive board about where they might curtail expenses, and she was frustrated that they were not taking her seriously. The only other problem she could think of was the wedding she performed perhaps a month ago. She said that as she was marrying the couple, an ex-girlfriend of the groom showed up and created a disturbance. She was appalled at the poor behavior on the part of the woman. Those were the only two instances she could think of when our victim had a moment of unhappiness."

"Did you ask her about Laura's husband?" Jill asked.

"Yeah, it's always the husband!" Brenda added.

Angela smiled at them and said, "Based on what the friend said, we can take the husband off our list. They were deeply in love and had great respect for each other's personalities and needs throughout the day. Jennifer said it was the most perfect marriage she ever had a chance to view from the outside looking in."

"Did she know the name of the crazy woman who interrupted the wedding ceremony?" Jill asked.

"She did not know. It was just a story that Laura relayed to her. She said that as far as she knew, all of the weddings were described in the local paper, and we could look it up there as it is custom to list who officiated the ceremony. The friend said that Laura didn't officiate very many weddings."

After Jill finished digesting the results of Angela's interview, she asked, "Do we need to stick around here? Or do we think we've gotten as much information as we can about Laura from people who knew her well."

"I think we're done here, especially as Laura and her husband typically attended the first service. I don't think we'd learn anything new from the parishioners attending the second service, just more confirmation about what we already learned," Angela said, and Brenda nodded in agreement. They decided to head back to the hotel to see what new information Marie might have found.

CHAPTER 11

When the three women returned to the hotel, they noticed new information had been added to the paper. Jill looked at her watch and realized she had about six more hours with her friends before they departed for their homes. This might be their last brainstorming session with everyone in the same room.

Marie had added information about their victim, the catering staff, and the victim's family. Jill's mother had a separate page on ways that a killer could source fentanyl gas. Jo verified that the church was in trouble financially, but their victim Laura Locklear had no financial issues; she and her husband managed well on the income the two of them earned. Equally important, Nathan and Charles were keeping the group fed and hydrated while they researched.

They still had a few mysteries to run down. They had no video footage of the road yet. The mysterious stranger who was parked near the church ruin might be nothing, or then again might be the key to the case. Then there was the crazy woman they needed to track down who had disrupted the earlier wedding. Angela began scanning the local newspaper's wedding announcements to find the couple Laura had officiated for and to get the disruptive woman's name.

"Mom, tell us about fentanyl."

"Oh boy, where to start? Let me talk about sources first. You can get fentanyl pills and patches by prescription at any pharmacy. You can buy real and synthetic fentanyl pills on the street. You can also purchase the chemicals that make fentanyl and make it yourself. So somebody who wants it bad enough can find it. Let me move on to how you aerosolize it. You can't get a prescription for gaseous fentanyl. However, you could take something like an olive oil spritzer, and you can mix powdered fentanyl with water. Or you can take a fentanyl patch and scrape off its contents and put that in your spritzer."

"So, our killer might have had access to patches. Let's talk about how this might've gone down. If someone was pointing an oil spritzer at me, I wouldn't just stand there and inhale. I would immediately hold my breath and turn away and move to a safe distance. Especially if this was a complete stranger or somebody I thought might be a whack job," Jill said.

"I have no idea how I would react. I would be so startled by someone's behavior toward me that I might just stand there while my brain tried to figure out what was going on," Jo commented.

"If it was someone I knew and they said they wanted me to smell something—perfume, air freshener—I would likely stand there and sniff the air. If I did sniff the air and the drug hit me, I might not notice that the person trying to harm me has put a patch on my skin. I'm curious about how she arrived at her final resting spot in the vineyard," Angela said.

"Okay, my friends, you are a little more cooperative than I am with people doing strange things around me. To your question, Angela—there's no indication that she was dragged there. I didn't see marks in the soil and her shoes were on her feet. You would think your shoes would fall off if you were dragged somewhere. Laura was wearing low pumps, and there's no way they would stay on if she had been dragged. I could be wrong, but it looked to me like she just fell asleep in the vineyard, which would be the effect of an overdose of fentanyl. Somehow the killer got her to walk into a certain row in the vineyard. Perhaps the person wanted Laura to see the grapes, except that it's October and the grapes would've been harvested in the summertime, I think. Nathan, maybe you know this grape-growing region better than I do."

"It's likely they harvest most grapes in August and September here due to the higher altitude. So, it's possible that someone would think that there are grape clusters on a vine worth looking at, or if they know nothing about grapes, they might not understand that there is a harvest time," Nathan replied.

Jill nodded and asked her mother to stand.

"I want to pretend that Mom is Laura Locklear and I'm the killer," Jill said as she positioned her mother in their sitting room. She grabbed a canvas bag and hung it onto her shoulder.

"Hey Laura, did you know there are grape clusters down in that vineyard?" Jill said, pointing to where Nathan was standing in their efficiency kitchen. She walked over there and waved her Mom to come closer.

"I know I'm a bad actress, Mom, but just run with it," Jill said when she saw her mother had not moved.

Once her mom got closer, Jill pulled a bottle of olive oil out of the canvas bag and made a fake spraying sound. And then she grabbed a piece of plastic wrap from the kitchen and slapped that on her mother's arm.

"Laura, are you feeling tired or sleepy? You want to sit down here in the sun and take a nap?"

Her mother finally understood her role and sat down next to a kitchen cabinet. Jill made another fake spraying sound. Her mother obediently closed her eyes and sagged to her side as though asleep. Jill mimicked putting a few more patches on her mother's arms.

Finally she reached down and checked her mom's pulse, and with a poorly acted evil laugh said, "There, now you're dead!"

"I would applaud your awful acting job, but you really shouldn't kill your mother, especially during your wedding weekend," Nathan said.

"Yes, but could Laura's murder have happened that way? There were no signs of a struggle. That says to me that she willingly walked over to where she was eventually found lying dead."

"I'd say it's possible. If that's the way it happened, Laura must have known her killer. Even in broad daylight, I wouldn't follow a complete stranger into a vineyard. It's just too strange a conversation to contemplate," Marie said. "If I lived in this area like she did, once the wedding was over, I would head home and do other things. I wouldn't stand in a vineyard admiring grapes that I might not care about."

"We know this murder was premeditated. The killer somehow aerosolized fentanyl and had access to fentanyl patches. This took planning. He or she likely scraped the fentanyl on the patch for use as an aerosol. That says your killer is organized and quite capable of higher thought. As to who Laura followed into the vineyard, to me that says she was being respectful or kind to the killer. There's nothing in the scenario that says the killer is male or female. However, this is a form of poisoning, so I would argue that it's more likely your killer is female," Melissa said. "A female likely would have gotten victim's guard down more than a male."

Jill hadn't thought of the poisoning angle with the fentanyl, but once Melissa with her criminal psychologist knowledge looked at the situation, Jill knew she was right with her assessment.

"Wow, Melissa, that was helpful. So I need to look at this

homicide as poisoning. Our analysis is so clear that I can't help but think our killer is a female. Let's run down that path for a while. If we look at our pool of suspects on the board, who do we have that we haven't spoken to who should rise to the top of our suspect list because of their gender?"

"A few of the employees from the bakery, the wife of the vineyard owner, the unknown woman in the car, and the secretary at the church who recommended Laura. Anyone else? And the ex-girlfriend from the previous wedding," Marie suggested.

"All of the ladies in this room," Jo said.

"Remember, I'm the only person Laura knew, so I'm the only person who could be a suspect."

"Besides the fact that you don't have what it takes to be a killer, I think all of us could personally vouch that you were not missing from the reception for a long enough time to kill our victim," Melissa said.

"Melissa, you made my day by saying that I don't have what it takes to be a killer. It's against everything I stand for and why I continue to consult on these cases. I look at the tragedy of Laura's life cut short. Then there's the impact on her immediate family. I don't think you ever get over having a close family member murdered."

"Of the people you named, I've done a search on everyone except the mysterious stranger in the car and the ex-girlfriend. In summary, there's nothing on the surface that screams 'I hate Laura Locklear enough to murder her.' I'll be back at work tomorrow, but as soon as you find out who your mysterious woman is, drop an email to me and I'll check her out," Marie said.

"Charles and I are going to stay the next day and a half in case we can help Jill solve this case," Brenda said. She'd told Jill and Angela earlier, but now she let the larger group know their change in plans.

"I have time to interview a few more people today," Angela said. "If they're willing to be interviewed on a Sunday."

"I've gone as far as I can with your victim's and her church's financials," Jo said. "I'll check out the groom of the couple that Laura married prior to your wedding. I'll look for something that would've angered another woman enough that she tried to interrupt his wedding."

"Yeah, the woman who interrupted the wedding was strange. I'm speculating, but presumably the groom had dropped her months ago when he took up with the woman he eventually married. That's a long time to stay mad enough that you want to kill someone, but crazier things have happened," Jill said. "I think I might invite the detective over here to look at the information we've collected. He might have some more test results from the autopsy that tell us something."

"Like what?" Barbara asked.

"Depending on how sophisticated their lab is, they may be able to give a report on what the fentanyl was mixed with or whether it was a real or synthetic drug. I don't know that changes who were looking at as a suspect, but it would be interesting information."

Jill looked at her watch and calculated when about half of the room would need to leave for the airport. She was running out of time.

"Angela, why don't you complete your final interviews, and everyone else who has to leave tonight could take a break right now and pack your bags and check out if you haven't already done so. Or maybe you don't want to work on this case and would like to take some time to get to see a little more of Asheville. That's perfectly fine, and I wouldn't want to deny you the opportunity to see a different part of the United States."

She stepped into the kitchen and grabbed a bottle of fizzy water to rehydrate after talking so much. She looked up and no one had moved except Angela, who was heading out the door to interview Jess Redmond's wife and the caterers if she could find them.

"We're here to serve you and Nathan. We're happy you guys finally tied the knot, and we like the woman who married you. We'll use every bit of time left to help you find her killer," Jo said.

Jill's eyes watered over the love and friendship she felt coming from her friends. She was really lucky to know these people, and she had to go around and individually hug each of them.

"On that happy note, I'll see if I can get the detective to visit before everybody disperses home. That way, if he has questions all the right people are in the room."

She placed a call to the detective and explained where she was in regard to the investigation and the fact that her team-mates were leaving in a few hours. She invited him to their hotel suite and he said he'd be there in less than thirty minutes.

CHAPTER 12

*N*athan and Charles created a big lunch so that everyone left their wedding weekend with a full belly. Of course, he paired it with perfect wines. The detective joined them for the meal, though he stood with his plate and read the everybody's notes that were taped to the wall. He imbibed in the wine, announcing that he was off-duty that day but was hoping to gain some new information on the puzzling case.

"Detective, do you have any new test results from the autopsy that you can share with me?" Jill asked.

"Dr. Baker swabbed Laura Locklear's arms and they tested positive for the drug. She said that both the inhaled drug and the drug delivered by patch tested out to be medical-grade fentanyl rather than a synthetic derivative."

"So, our killer obtained the product from a pharmacy, rather than a street corner. When we catch her, we should be able to find out where she got the medication. How about road cameras? Did your department make contact with any of the residents along the road to the church ruin?"

"It's Sunday, so the department doesn't have the resources to contact those homeowners. We just have a skeletal crew on the weekends. I have a police explorer kid here tomorrow that I plan to assign running down the security footage. She's a geek and can probably walk any homeowner through creating a tape to send to us. I don't know if this research is going to yield anything, and if the homeowner doesn't know how to transfer video feed to us, then I'm no help."

"Got it. Wise decision. So we mostly think our killer is a female. This death by fentanyl wouldn't require the killer be strong or tall. It's a way of poisoning someone."

"Where did they get the fentanyl gas, though? That's a big clue that could lead us to the killer as it is hard to obtain."

"Not necessarily. We did a poorly acted re-enactment of the murder. My mother is a retired chemist. She believes that the killer could have aerosolized the drug, using something as simple as an olive oil spritzer."

"I'm not much of a chef, so I don't own any spritzer. What are you talking about?" Detective Parnell said.

"Here's a picture of the item from a website. Basically, you put a liquid of your choice in it, give it a few pumps, and voilà, your fentanyl is in the air.

"Let me watch the poorly acted re-enactment. It might stir some ideas."

Jill rolled her eyes but did as the detective asked. Her mother followed directions better this time and tried to throw her own spin on the few lines that she had.

"The visualization helps. By the way, you're all weird to put so much energy into solving this crime, rather than enjoying the tourist attractions of this area."

"We wouldn't have it any other way. Jill's wedding officiant deserves to have her case solved. We can always come back to Asheville, but we can't always solve Laura Locklear's murder," Marie said.

"True. I must say that your re-enactment might be close to the truth. So who is on your list of female suspects?"

Jill wondered if the detective was humoring her or if he really saw Jill and her team as part of the solution to this homicide.

"Any of the female attendees to my wedding, the vineyard owner's wife, any female catering staff, any random female who drove by the church in the time around her death, and the upset ex-girlfriend."

"That's not a small number of people."

"No, but I don't really think it is any of my friends who attended the wedding. They have no motive, nor do I think that Laura would have followed a random friend out to the vineyard. None of us have been prescribed fentanyl, and despite this well-stocked kitchen, there isn't an olive oil spritzer. Of course, they could have lied, but then I can't remember anyone being gone for longer than the few minutes it takes for a bathroom break. None of my friends smoke, so they didn't step out for a cigarette break. The killer would have needed to stay with Laura for about twenty minutes to make sure she was pulseless."

"So that leaves Mrs. Redmond, who by the way mostly has an alibi; the catering staff; and a random female driver from the road if we are only concerned about female suspects," the detective concluded.

"Yes. Angela from my team is on her way to interview Mrs. Redmond and try to find the final two catering staff. We've interviewed the other two. Angela found the names of the couple from the newspaper that Laura Locklear officiated at when an unidentified female appeared and tried to disrupt the wedding. Marie is reviewing the groom's social media feed to find the name of the woman. If we can't get her name from there, Angela was going to call the couple."

"Have you finished researching the church?" the detective asked.

Jill looked to Jo for the answer.

"Not entirely. The church is in financial distress. They were having declining membership before the pandemic and were granted a reprieve from making hard decisions thanks to government loans. I'm looking at the hard decisions now and who supported them or not. I should have a chart available on strategies and supporters before I leave in a few hours."

"Okay, are we all caught up in sharing information?" Jill asked. She received nods of agreement from everyone and turned to the detective.

"What other information are you waiting on, Detective? What are your thoughts on Laura's killer?"

A variety of emotions coursed through the detective. They ranged from *Who the heck did these civilians think they were asking him to share the information he collected, to OMG I don't have any additional case information beyond what these civilians have already collected.*

Jill was getting used to shell-shocked law enforcement officers metering their responses to her. So she prompted, "Did any of your interviews reveal new information or confirm what we already collected?"

"We have interviewed the victim's husband twice. As I mentioned before, he has a verified alibi that he was hundreds of miles away at the time of her death. In a second interview, we questioned him about her enemies or people that had made her unhappy. Basically, it's the same information you found during your interviews. Laura Locklear was unhappy with the management of the church. Her husband said that she felt that they were not taking the financial problems seriously enough and weren't trying to cut back on spending. We asked him what he thought about the church's spending. He said he also was concerned, and given his occupation he could see the steps they needed to take to fix their budget. However, he's been very busy at work recently and didn't have the time to take on the church elders.

"Based on what I've heard from you folks today, we'll make another run at interviewing him tomorrow. I want to know more about the young lady who disrupted the wedding that our victim last officiated at. We need to add her to our suspect list," Detective Parnell said. "I'll have someone from my office stop by to speak to the couple. We need to talk to them to verify the name of the woman. We don't want to take a guess at the woman's name by examining social media feed."

Marie gave the detective a look of disappointment. She debated saying something, but then she thought about the fact they were working with two different standards. She could tell that in a court of law, saying that you found something in a social media post would be considered light evidence and they would want stronger verification of the woman's identity. It would be a weird discussion with the young newlyweds and likely better handled by the police. She was leaving soon, but Jill would keep them updated on the case. Still, she decided she would check the woman's social media posts anyway to see if there was anything interesting there. When they first discovered the woman's story, they all agreed that someone willing to interrupt a wedding was a person who wasn't mentally right.

"Well, thanks for the update," the detective said.

"Detective, I'd like to join your intern as she searches for video feed along the road to the church ruin. You met Henrik Klein at the wedding, and my laptop has software with his advanced facial recognition system. If I work in tandem with your intern, we can identify drivers much more quickly."

The detective gave a pained grimace as he thought about Jill's request. He would have to check in with his department to understand if there were any legal issues with having a civilian work in tandem with his department.

"Let me check with the department leadership to make sure we're not violating any laws by having you there. I'll text you an answer one way or the other," the detective said as he departed the hotel suite.

CHAPTER 13

$\mathcal{A}$ngela returned to the suite announcing that she had interviewed Mrs. Redmond and an additional member of the catering staff.

"I was going to interview the final member of the catering staff, but I think the timing is wrong on that person. I also wanted to get back here before everyone leaves. I have a few hugs to give out."

"What did you learn?" Marie asked.

"We can take Mrs. Redman off our suspect list. She was in town at the time of Laura's death."

"Yeah, that's what the detective said," Jill said.

"However, I did learn some new information. Mrs. Redman knew Laura Locklear, as they both were members of the historical society. She liked Laura and agreed with her opinions, which didn't sit well with all members of the society."

"Why?" Jo asked.

"She seems to have ruffled some feathers regarding the portrayal of slavery and Asheville's role in the Civil War. Some members believe that slavery occurred over such a small period of time in Asheville's history, that it needn't be mentioned.

94

Laura, as a history major in college, had a vastly different opinion. Some members of the historical society had an interest in history, but not necessarily an education. They had a fixed idea of what happened. Laura would suggest books to reference her statements, but it would fall on deaf ears. So that led to a lot of angst between Laura and some committee members. I asked Mrs. Redmond if she thought that any of that angst was enough to cause Laura's murder, and she didn't think so. Though she fully admitted that she didn't know what it took to kill somebody since she had no personal knowledge of someone who murdered."

"I'd have to agree with Mrs. Redmond that a disagreement over the history of certain events in Asheville is unlikely to inspire someone to murder. Denial of history by itself does not meet any mental health standard found in the *Diagnostic and Statistical Manual of* Mental Disorders, which is the preeminent book in my field," Melissa said.

"Thanks. It's good to have you on our team so we don't chase people who can only be weakly viewed as suspects. How about the caterer? Any new information there?"

"No. She was on the late shift for your wedding and had left just before Rachel called her husband to help her carry stuff to her car. This employee turned left out of the church ruin and was parked on the grass. She said she made her own parking space in the lot. She didn't notice if there was a car across the street. When she left the wedding reception, she was running late for another appointment and was talking on her phone as she got into the car. She also said that Elizabeth left perhaps thirty to forty-five minutes before she did. So our stranger in the car was likely gone by then as there was no reason to wait around. Also, the woman I interviewed said that the other person that worked the wedding left a few minutes after her, so I'll put her on my list of people to interview if we have no clues from anyone else."

"I think you're right not to pursue interviewing the fourth catering staff person. I think we're likely done with researching all the angles that we can for this case. Jo is putting the finishing touches on her analysis of the church. I hope to get some driveway camera footage tomorrow that perhaps will give us some new clues. Mr. and Mrs. Conroy are staying behind to help me. Nathan and Angela will be off filming the countryside tomorrow and the rest of you leave tonight."

"I have some fresh cookies paired with a local wine for everyone to enjoy before they depart," Nathan said, passing out wine glasses while his father followed with a tray of cookies.

Angela stood up and held her wineglass up, "To Jill and Nathan, my friends and employers. May this be the first of many weekends of love, friendship, family, and food. Sláinte!"

There was a clanking of glasses all around and further toasts to the marriage of Jill and Nathan.

"Where are you guys going to live?" Marie asked.

"I'll be moving into Jill's house. She needs to be near her vines and her chemistry analyzers. She also has a superb security system to protect her. I'll continue to work on my property, but lease the house out as a vacation rental," Nathan said.

"Is Arthur moving to Jill's house?" Jo asked about the cat that didn't get along with Jill's dog, Trixie.

"We haven't checked in with him to see what he prefers. We'll do that when we get back."

"How will you do that? One meow is a 'yes' and two meows are a 'no'?" Angela said.

"We'll see if he acclimates to Jill's property. With the barn and vineyard, he should find things to peak his interests. But if he seems unhappy, I'll have him stay at my office and he can wander around his current cat kingdom."

"I like that you're going to let the cat decide. Does he like you, Jill?" Jo asked.

"It depends on if Trixie is with me. He loves me when I'm by myself and shuns me when the dog is with me."

"Has Arthur saved your life?" Angela asked.

"Not yet. I think it's easier for a dog to save your life than a cat."

"Jill, you've been keeping stuff from me. When did your dog save your life?" Barbara asked.

"It was one of my early cases, Mom. Angela was staying with me at the time and a Russian sniper would have killed me if Trixie hadn't urged me to move. That sniper is dead, so you don't have to worry about my safety."

"After watching you with this case, I'm thinking there's a lot you haven't told me. I didn't know you needed a fancy security system. Why did you get one?"

"My residence has been attacked multiple times and the security system has given us enough warning to take on the bad guys. Besides, you know that Nathan is a black belt, so he's my backup security system and that's working well."

"Maybe you should retire from the business of solving murders if it's that dangerous," Barbara said with a worried look on her face.

"Mom, this is why I don't tell you about some of our misadventures. Law enforcement is pretty good about coming to our aid no matter where we are in the world. I enjoy bringing justice to the recently departed and their families, as do many of the people in this room. At the very least, we have a sizable vacation bank account built up from these cases as most people pay us for our time and effort. This case with Laura Locklear is a freebie because she did such a wonderful job at our wedding."

"Mrs. Quint, I'll admit that several times I've been scared by the nasty people who are chasing us, but Jill is right; law enforcement always comes to our aid, and we feel really good about sending the real killer to jail," Jo said.

"Frankly, Jill will tell you that I get a secret thrill every time I get to use my martial arts skills against people who would do her harm. I've watched people attack her about once a quarter and she is a survivor, and they have ended up dead or in jail. It's part of the reason I love her, and I wouldn't change a thing," Nathan said.

"Oh Sweetie, that's so romantic. I love you too."

Jo, Marie, and Angela joined in a group hug. Jill's mom threw her hands up in the air realizing she was outnumbered.

"I hate to break up this romantic hug-a-thon, but it's time I left for the airport. It's a long ride back to California," Melissa said.

There were murmurs from others as there were many people heading for the airport. Within fifteen minutes, Jo, Marie, Melissa, Jill's mom, and Nathan's brother all left to catch flights home. Jill, Nathan, Angela, and Nathan's parents were left once the suite door closed on the last set of departing friends.

"So, Jill, what are we doing tomorrow to solve this case?" Brenda asked.

"I'm waiting to hear back from the detective as to whether I can work with his intern to get footage of the road to the church. If the detective decides not to invite me to join his intern, I think we'll make another trip to the ruin and stop and ask the residents ourselves. If he does allow me to observe the intern, then I'll be there when video footage comes in that might identify who might be the killer. As there are likely multiple cars on the road, I'll text the names to you as I find them, and you can start researching these people. When we were looking for evidence on the road, a car passed us about every three to five minutes. That means that I'll have some twenty cars to research for the period around Laura's death. Does that sound like a plan?"

Her new mother-in-law looked nervous and pleased at her role for the next day. Marie had left some instructions for her to follow, but she'd never done anything like this before. "I've never done this before, so you'll have to bear with me tomorrow. Marie left instructions that I hope to follow, but I won't be as fast or thorough as she is."

"I appreciate your help no matter how slow you'll be. Two heads are better than one when working on solving these cases. In the past, I didn't always have the full time and attention of Jo, Marie, or Angela as they have day jobs they have to attend to. I'll start digging into financial information myself if Jo can't give me time, and trust me when I say that's a foreign language for me. We'll divide our suspects into two groups. Those who are driving a dark mid-sized SUV and are female and everyone else. We'll want to concentrate on the females first."

"Okay. When should I plan on starting work?"

"I don't know yet. I'm assuming the intern will start at seven or eight in the morning. She'll need to understand the assignment. She'll need to know how to reach the owners of the houses that we saw with cameras. Then she'll have to talk them through sending video coverage to her. I'm thinking we won't have a need for you or me to research individuals until at least nine in the morning. How does that sound?"

"That's sounds fine. I'm more of a morning person than my son, but I'm not the morning lark that you are, Jill."

Jill laughed and replied, "I don't know if I've ever met someone as allergic to morning as Nathan. When we're traveling or working on a case my friends and I plan to deal with a zombie if we need Nathan before nine in the morning."

"Hey, I heard that," Nathan said.

"If the zombie description fits, then you must wear it."

Jill looked around and everyone was smiling over the long-running discussion of Nathan's inability to be lucid early in the morning.

"At least I'm wide awake whenever Jill needs saving. An

adrenaline rush is all I need to change costumes from zombie to mixed martial arts fighter in a matter of seconds."

"That you do, Sweetie. Whenever we're in danger, Nathan snaps to attention like he just breathed in caffeine."

"Nathan, Barbara was worried about Jill's safety; maybe I should also be worried about your safety. Just how dangerous have these cases been? Have you been held at gunpoint? Has someone flashed a knife at you?" Brenda asked.

"Mom, the next time you and Dad visit us in California, I'll do a demonstration for you of my martial arts skills. As you termed it, I have had a knife flashed at me which I kicked out of the assailant's hand. Jill and I have been chased through the bayous by gunmen in Louisiana. We faced down the Russian mob in Québec, and most recently an arsonist who planned to light Jill's house on fire. Despite all of those adventures, I don't have so much as a hair out of place on my head. Jill and her team don't try to go at it alone to solve these cases. They always bring in local law enforcement, who have always been there when we're facing down the worst of these criminals. You don't need to worry about my safety."

"Son, you're not making your mother comfortable with that explanation. I hear what you say, though, and we're probably better off not knowing about all the scrapes you get into with your bride."

"I'll keep that in mind, Dad. When we talk on the phone, I'll tell you about the wine business. It's fascinating to me, though I must say that Jill's cases are fascinating as well."

"Mrs. Conroy, I've been in some tough positions with Jill on some of these cases. In fact, I was actually shot on a golf course in one of Jill's cases. Fortunately, it was a superficial wound that didn't even require stitches. That was probably ten cases ago. I admit I'm a justice junkie just like Jill. We've met some wonderful families who've lost someone they loved to a murderer. So, no matter the danger that we put ourselves in at times, the outcome is always worth it," Angela said with a smile.

"If that explanation was supposed to make me feel better, it didn't work. Still, I understand what all of you are up to in solving these cases. Laura Locklear is the first person I've known who was murdered. I don't want her death to go unsolved. I want the murderer caught and sent to prison for a very long time. I'm so sorry that with each anniversary that you mark, you'll likely think of Laura as well."

"Yes, we will think of Laura and the simple beauty she added to our wedding. We'll honor her every year on our anniversary," Nathan said.

"Maybe we could think of something to honor her with so that her life doesn't go unnoticed. Maybe if the Redmonds start using the ruin as an event space, they could name it after Laura given that she was a history buff. Or maybe I could name a future vintage after her. Of course, I can't remember if she even liked wine, so I'll have to talk to her husband to find a suitable way to permanently honor her role in our lives," Jill said.

CHAPTER 14

*N*athan closed the door as the last person exited. He and Angela had a schedule to follow tomorrow to gain the pictures he needed for his new clients. Then she would fly home to Wisconsin tomorrow evening. He sank down on the sofa in their hotel suite's living room and slung his arm around Jill's shoulders.

"If you had asked me in the seconds following my proposal last week how I envisioned this weekend going, my description would have failed by quite a margin," Nathan said.

"Sweetie, I'm right there with you. I had flashes of you in your beautiful tux, me in a suitable dress, and a long weekend of partying with our friends. I never would have imagined that someone so close to us and our wedding would end up being murdered. Nor would I ever imagine that our mothers would be so interested in helping solve the case. After the fact that Laura was murdered, perhaps the most shocking thing was seeing my mom happily contributing to researching where to buy fentanyl."

"How about my mom? She extended her stay here specifically so she could help you on this case. I appreciate how respectful you've been in your interactions with her on the case. She has no visible skills that I can remember that would help with these investigations, yet you've managed to make her feel so worthy that she extended their visit by two days. A guy couldn't ask for more out of his new bride and her relationship with his mother."

"You should've seen the look Angela gave me when your mother first said she was going to extend their stay so she could help me. Angela's eyes said, *Accept her offer graciously*, which I was going to do, by the way, but it was hard to avoid the thought beam that Angela was directing at me to say *yes*. Your mother genuinely wants to help on the case and she hasn't slowed down our progress. She's not volunteering on this case over celebrity, or arrogance, or entertainment; rather, she's helping because she feels bad for the victim and that's all I can ask of anyone who joins my team even on a temporary basis."

"You don't think she'll ask to be part of your team permanently?" Nathan asked, curious about how Jill was reading his mother.

"I don't think so. She's rather uncomfortable with the investigation. She's an introvert. I think she knows she's better off not knowing what danger my cases drag you into. Also, she knew Laura briefly and liked her and liked the job she did at our wedding. She wouldn't have that personal connection in my future cases. I think she'll be one and done. She already feels the pressure to perform as well as Marie does with her background checks. She needs to ignore that pressure as it's a losing battle. Marie is a professional who has been seeking information on individuals for over twenty years. No matter how good your mother is, she'll be unable to live up to Marie's level of investigating people, and I'm totally fine with that."

"I'm impressed with how well you understand my mother and her motivations and needs, and I think you're right that she'll be a one-and-done participant on your team. On happier news, Angela and I have our day planned out before she returns to Wisconsin. We have a lot of pictures to collect of two wineries, their staff, their vines, and all the other angles I need to make beautiful marketing materials. We're taking her suitcase with us so if we fall short of time, we won't have to come back to the hotel to collect her luggage before heading to the airport. We checked the weather forecast, and fortunately, Mother Nature is cooperating with us."

"I hope the detective calls back with approval for me to observe his intern. If he doesn't, I'll be twiddling my thumbs and possibly ringing the doorbells of homeowners along the road to the ruin. We weren't very successful the first time we did that."

"You can join Angela and me as we roam over two wineries."

"I'd be too distracted thinking about this case. I'd be a wet blanket on your day."

"You're never a wet blanket, but I hear what you're saying. I'm taking our rental car; do we need another one for you?'

"I hadn't thought that far ahead. It depends on my day. If I'm simply going to the police station, it's cheaper to take a car service there. If I have to head out to do my own sleuthing, it makes sense to rent a car."

Jill heard her phone sound with a text and reached forward to the coffee table to pick it up. She and Nathan read the text together and a smile crossed her face.

"It looks like a car service is going to fulfill my needs tomorrow. Actually, if Angela's awake at eight in the morning, I'll have her drop me off. There's no reason for you to wake up early to give me a ride when you have a very busy day ahead of you."

Jill sent a text off to Angela and got a quick reply for her ride the next morning.

"Well, that's all set. I've been thinking about modifications to my house to make it our home and for you to be more comfortable. What would you say about taking charge of redoing my kitchen and remodeling the main bedroom so there's adequate closet space for you? When I bought the house, I gave no thought to someone living there with me, and as I think about it, the house needs some renovation. Should we install a cat door for Arthur? I want him to feel welcome in his new home."

"Arthur would appreciate a cat door. Especially if it was one that Trixie can't use. It's an easy fix as I think we can just swap doors between the two houses. I'm thinking of your back door by the laundry. Like you told the group earlier, Arthur will find things that he likes about your house more than mine, including the chance to stalk new vermin and birds. Just as soon as he starts ruling the roast over Trixie, I think he'll be happy at our new home."

"That doesn't bode well for my dog, but after watching the two of them for over three years, I have to agree with your assessment. Will you need to do anything to your house for it to become a rental? I would think it would be wildly popular for people to live in the central valley wine region."

"I'm fond of some of my furniture, so we'll have to negotiate the marriage of our two households when we return."

"I'll be very flexible with the furniture marriage. I care about my barn full of analyzers and my office and not much else."

"I thought that might be your feelings about the situation. I'll work out some sketches of interiors for both the renovation and our furniture marriage. I thought that you wouldn't have strong preferences for your house beyond your office, and that will make our joint households much easier to merge," Nathan said.

"I suppose it's weird for me to care more about my barns than my house."

"You can't care about everything as you only have so much brain space. Your not caring about the house makes the merger of our households so much easier than if we had completely different visions of our future home together. Frankly, I had counted on that when I gave thought to where we would live. You just lived up to my expectations."

"Now that I think about it, there are many practical things we need to talk about to merge our lives. You proposed, I accepted, we got married, but we haven't talked about our financial future. I suppose we need to set up a joint bank account to manage the house and boring stuff like that. Having waited to my mid-forties to marry for the first time will make some of these joint decisions awkward as I'm used to being solely in charge."

"I'm in the same boat as you, Jill. This is my first marriage also, you know, but we'll figure it out."

Jill rested her head against Nathan's shoulder and said, "I really do love you. You give me the freedom to be weird me, yet I can always feel your support even when you're not standing by my shoulder."

"You don't hassle me about being a zombie in the morning. Instead, you work your schedule around me. We share an interest in the wine business and I get to play Superman on occasion when you get into trouble on cases. What's not to love about that?"

"We're turning into sappy lovebirds the first week of our marriage."

"It was bound to happen sooner or later. We love how each of us handles the weird parts of our personalities."

"That's a deeply intuitive sentence. Have you spent time around Melissa undergoing psychoanalysis?"

Nathan laughed, "No, I'm just a sensitive guy."

"Well, my sensitive guy, let's head to bed."

CHAPTER 15

*J*ill smiled at her new mother-in-law, as she was coherent in the morning, unlike her son. Brenda joined her in the suite for breakfast before Angela arrived to drop Jill off at the police station. Jill tried to set Brenda at ease about doing her research as she identified drivers on the road to the church ruin.

"Don't worry about doing the same job as Marie. You're an extra set of hands to research while I stare at boring security footage. Whatever information you come up with will be better than what I have, okay?"

"I'll do my best."

Jill and Angela waved goodbye and left the suite. Twenty minutes later Angela left Jill at the curb of the main Asheville police station. It was an old and ugly dark red brick three-story building on a hilly street. The fire department was attached, and the Sheriff's department wasn't far away. Bricks were rarely used in Jill's native California as they didn't tolerate the move-ment from earthquakes much. Bricks were like shortbread cookies, and they disintegrated into crumbs. She entered the front office and asked for Detective Parnell. The receptionist said she would page him, and suggested Jill take a seat.

Jill sat down and pulled out her phone to play a word game. She was too distracted to do anything else. She looked up when she heard her name called.

"Hello, Detective," Jill said, standing up.

"Hello, Dr. Quint, please follow me."

Jill followed the detective behind a badge-accessed door and up a flight of stairs into a room with a bunch of cubicles. The detective stopped at one where there was a woman who looked to be about twenty. She was tapping away at a computer with a speed that Jill admired.

"Madison Lewis, meet Dr. Jill Quint," Detective Parnell introduced the two women. "I explained your role in Laura Locklear's death and what you want to do, so I'll leave you to it. Call me when you make identification of people."

With that last instruction, the detective left the cubicle room.

"Hello Madison, call me Jill. Did Detective Parnell explain what my role is here today?"

"He explained a little bit. He said you're a forensic pathologist and you just got married last Friday. He and his fellow detectives are trying to find the murderer who killed the woman who presided over your wedding ceremony."

"Okay, that's a good start. I have a team and we do private consultations on murder around the world. I perform autopsies and my friends conduct interviews, analyze social media, and review the finances of anyone who's dead. When I'm not doing that, I own a vineyard in California. I brought my laptop with me which has a sophisticated facial identity program on it. As soon as you get video footage of any driver on the road during the time that Laura was murdered, I'm going to run it through my program to try to identify him or her. Someone back at my hotel is going to begin researching each name that we come up with here. We're specifically interested in women about your age in a dark midsize SUV, but we will be researching everyone."

"Okay, that's pretty cool. I'm thinking about a law enforcement career, but the route you've taken sounds far more interesting. Does it pay well?"

"The autopsies or the vineyard?"

"Both, I guess."

"Well, if you want to do autopsies, Madison, you'll need to go to medical school and that's not cheap and it's a long education. After you graduate, you can be hired by a hospital or a state or county government and work as a medical examiner or coroner. Depending on your state, it may pay well. If you want to grow grapes, then you should get some education in viticulture and enology. Viticulture is the study of grapevines and enology is the study of winemaking."

"Can I intern with you? Your jobs sound fascinating."

"I don't have an internship to offer. I'm a forensic pathologist and private investigator and winemaker. Why don't we start by looking for video footage of the road and you'll get a sense of how I work."

Jill liked inspiring the next generation to go into her two chosen fields of study, but at the moment she had a murder to solve. Maybe if she liked the work that Madison did for her on this case, she would invite her out to California for her to see the duality of her two jobs. She would really need a case that was based in California, but recently her cases had taken her to many places. She would park that idea in the back of her brain and act on it later.

"Sure. The detective said that you found video cameras on three driveways that you thought would capture traffic on the road. He gave me the addresses and I looked up the owners. I'm going to call them now and see if we can get them to cooperate."

Jill listened in as Madison began calling the homeowners.

With the first two houses, she clearly got a voicemail. On the third address, she struck pay dirt.

"Hello, is this Mrs. Williams?"

Madison got an affirmative response to her question.

"This is Madison Lewis with the Asheville Police Department. I'm assisting a detective on a case. We notice that you have a camera at the entrance to your home. Would you by chance still have the video from last Friday afternoon?"

Jill could tell from Madison's side of the conversation that the woman who answered the phone didn't know a thing about her video system. She put Madison on hold while she looked for someone else to answer Madison's questions.

A new person joined the conversation on the homeowner's end and Madison repeated her explanation. She then settled into a technical discussion about the tape. In the end, she offered to go to the homeowner's house and help him make a copy. He agreed that it was the fastest way to get her the information she needed.

"Do you want to stay here or come with me to the homeowner's house?"

"I'll go with you. There's nothing I can do here without new information. Do you have access to a car?"

"Yes. I have to let the detective know I'm leaving and sign out a pool car. It's a drag to drive it and has the words community service on it, so I've always felt silly driving it. However, we're on official police business and it's better if they pay for the gas than me."

Jill followed Madison as she got the keys, and they left the building. She was wearing her Police Explorer uniform and that would add legitimacy to the homeowner.

"Madison, you'll need to introduce me to the homeowner. You can tell them that my name is Jill Quint and that I'm a private consultant to the department, which is all true. I think to tell the homeowners more information would open us up to a long conversation rather than giving us the video footage that we want."

"I can do that," Madison said, as she set up a driving app to take them to the address with the camera.

"Why are you doing a Police Explorer program? You don't seem sure that you want to pursue a law enforcement career."

"There are so many choices, and I don't know what I want to do with my future. I've briefly tried several internships and they haven't suited me. I'm really good with computers, but I don't want to work in IT and code all day. Personally, you have the most interesting combination of jobs I've ever heard of, and I would think that you would use a lot of computer research in your work. I'm fascinated by all the information that's available on the Internet if I just have a reason to search for it."

"Maybe being a private detective would suit you. Let me tell you about the work I've done on this case. I know Detective Parnell informed you that Laura Locklear was the officiant at my wedding on Friday. We found her lying on the dirt in one of the rows of vines in the vineyard next to the church ruin where my wedding and reception took place."

"Oh my gosh, he just told me you were working on her murder. What a bizarre circumstance. Tell me more."

"When we first found her lying in the dirt, she had no visible wounds; she was just dead, and the police did not initially rule her death as a homicide."

"Isn't every dead woman ever found in the vineyard a homicide?"

"Madison, I think you've watched too many horror flicks. I haven't mentioned how old she was, so she could have had a heart attack and passed out in the vineyard and died of chest pain."

"Oh. Why do you think she was murdered?"

"I'll start with feeding you some clues. She had no wounds or bruises on her body. She was in her early forties. She walked at a good pace and spoke in full sentences. She didn't grimace, nor act confused in the two times I met her before the ceremony and during my wedding ceremony. What does that tell you?"

"I don't know other than it doesn't seem by her age or behavior that she was ready to die."

"That's a nice non-medical way to say that. She's young, so a sudden heart attack is unlikely. The fact that she had no problem walking or talking says that her brain, lungs, and heart were functioning. The fact that she wasn't grimacing means that she wasn't in pain, which might be a sign of an impending heart attack or stroke. Those are all clues."

"So how did she die?"

Jill opened her mouth and then thought of confidentiality, and finally said, "I'm not sure I can tell you. It's something the detective should do within the policies of the department."

"Oh, c'mon, man. You can't leave me hanging not knowing the answer."

"We'll check with the detective later."

"Was she strangled?"

"What is the evidence at a scene of someone being strangled?"

"I don't know."

"You have lots to learn," Jill said as Madison turned into the driveway of one of the houses Jill had already identified as having a camera on the road.

Madison spoke to the entry speaker box and the gate swung open to admit them. The house couldn't be seen from the road and was quite grand when they reached a curve in the road and got their first glimpse.

"Wow, this is a big house even by Asheville standards."

"Yeah, now I understand the gate and camera. There must be things to protect in that house."

Madison parked and Jill reminded the young woman,

"Remember, I'm Jill, just a consultant to the case. Let your uniform do all the talking."

Madison nodded and rang the doorbell.

A man in khakis and a polo shirt answered. "Yes?"

"Hello, I'm Explorer Madison Lewis from the Asheville Police Department. I believe I spoke with you about twenty minutes ago if you're Mr. Williams."

"Indeed. Come in and I'll take you to our camera room."

He then stuck out his hand to Jill and said, "Who are you?"

"I'm a private consultant to the department, so I don't have a badge."

"I didn't know that the police department used consultants."

Darn, this man was a combination of smart and imperious. Jill debated where to go next and settled on, "I was in the area and loaned to them through the FBI. Just ignore me as Madison is doing all the work here."

He gave her a long look, then took them to a room that appeared to be an office with a desk and computer monitor.

"I'll bring up the security program. I believe you said you were looking for footage between 1:30 and 3:30 last Friday, correct?"

"Yes, Sir, that's correct. If you can bring up the footage on your system, I brought a flash drive from the department that I'll copy it on to and we'll get on our way and leave you to your day."

"What are you looking for on my tape?"

"We want to track all the people who drove down this road. One of them may be related to a crime that took place."

For all of his cooperation, Mr. Williams seemed to be hovering over their efforts to get a copy of his tape. Madison was smart and had it zipped into a smaller file and they were on their way in less than ten minutes. After they left the gate and turned on to the main road, they finally spoke.

"He was an odd man. Cooperative yet suspicious. Maybe he's

one of those citizens who need to see a male in a full-dress uniform to meet his idea of a cop," Madison said.

"Have you run into that type?" Jill asked curiously.

"Yep. I get that I'm nothing like a fully trained police officer, but I still contribute to policing in this community."

"Yes, you're helping solve this murder with your work. Don't let weirdos like that wreck your day. I've gotten sass for years for being a female physician. It's outside noise; just concentrate on doing a good job."

"Are you sure I can't intern for you?"

"Madison, my life vacillates between pruning grapevines and fertilizing acres of vines to dodging bullets from a hired killer. I can't predict when I'm going to have an exciting case. You could come to watch me work and end up literally watching weeds grow for a week. My work schedule is too unpredictable."

"Okay. How about if you call me when you get your next case in the United States? My dad has a small plane and can fly me to wherever your case is. I want to watch how you solve cases, then I'll make up my mind whether to be a cop, a coroner, or a private investigator. Deal?"

"Okay, deal. Leave me your personal contact information before I leave today."

"You bet. So, before we arrived at the Williams' house, you were about to explain why Laura Locklear might be considered a homicide."

"Actually, I wasn't going to tell you that as I don't know how much the department wants to be shared on that case. We'll check with the detective when we get back to see if he has any qualms about my sharing information with you."

"Okay. We'll stop by and talk to him on the way to my cubicle."

Jill sighed, caught between the younger woman's desire to understand the case and her own innate confidentiality regarding any case. When they stopped by the detective's cubicle, they found he was out in the field but was expected back in thirty minutes. Madison would have to sit on hot coals a while longer.

They began looking at the tape. Jill looked at the time and then fast-forwarded it until it reached the end of the time range they were examining. She counted twenty-three cars passing the cameras, including two entering the Williams driveway that they would discount for now. That left twenty-one cars for Brenda and Jill to research.

"I need you to focus on each of the twenty-one cars until you find the best frame to identify the driver."

"Why don't I just look up each car's license plate for you? I have access to that database."

"You could do that, but the owner of the car is not necessarily the driver, right?"

"Right. Especially if it's a rental."

"Exactly."

"Okay, I'll start with the plate, but also get you the best picture of the face."

"Perfect."

They worked in silence as a team compiling a list of drivers on the road. They were both lost in their work and jumped when Detective Parnell said, behind them, "You had a question for me?"

Jill looked over her shoulder and said, "Yeah, I wasn't sure how many details of the murder I could share with Madison."

"Given that your entire wedding reception knows the details of this case, I'd say that horse left the barn long ago. Madison, as you should remember during your orientation as an intern, you'll hear confidential information at work every day. Dr. Quint can share the details of the murder with you, but you can't discuss those details with anyone outside of this department. Got it?"

"Yes, Sir," Madison said, and then she looked at Jill and said,

"You stopped your story about this case with the statement that she had no visible wounds, appeared to be in good health, and in the hour preceding her death reflected no pain. So, how did she die?"

"You're the wannabe detective; what's your guess of why she died?" the detective asked.

"I would say that she overdosed, but nothing that you told me about Laura Locklear sounds like she was either suicidal or a drug user."

"You're getting closer, Madison. I'm sure Jill will walk you through it. Call me if you need me," the detective said with a smile as he retreated to his own space.

"She died of an overdose of fentanyl, but why would we label this a homicide instead of an accidental overdose?" Jill showed her a picture of Laura lying in the dirt before her body was removed by the coroner.

"Let me think about your question while I find a few more drivers."

She gave Jill the owner of the vehicle and pictures of five more cars before she asked her next question.

"Was there drug paraphernalia near her body? Did you find pills in her stomach? They would still be there if she died three hours after ingesting them, right?"

"That's very good, Madison. You should always be suspicious of the scene with an overdose victim when there's no evidence of what they overdosed on. Overdoses are very unpredictable, and I've never seen a case where a person intended to kill themselves via drugs and didn't leave some kind of evidence behind. Either evidence that they snorted a drug, a syringe, or pills in their stomach should always be present. As you can see from that picture, we had none of that, and further, there was no evidence of pills in her stomach or her urine as we learned from her autopsy."

Madison had been able to multitask and provided Jill with

three more names while Jill took her through the explanation of the crime scene.

"Why is urine important and how do you know she overdosed if you didn't find pills in her stomach?"

"When someone takes an overdose of medication, it first gets into their blood. If they die quickly, the drug doesn't have time to reach their kidneys and be filtered into their urine. She had a fatal level of the drug in her blood. Of course, it could make it into the urine if the person is a regular user of a drug and isn't a one-and-done drug user. We searched her skin during the autopsy for a sign of an injection site on her body and found none. We swabbed her arms and face, and they were positive for fentanyl. So what does that mean?"

Jill watched as Madison was doing an admirable job of multitasking. Her hands were moving over the keyboard finding cars while her brain was mulling over what Jill said. Jill was using Henrik's software to identify the driver where they had a good picture. She was noting each person's identity on her list of suspects and forwarding the information to Brenda back at the hotel.

"Did she inhale it?" Madison asked.

"Yes, but what else happened?"

Finally, the intern shrugged and said, "I don't know."

"Fentanyl is a prescription drug that comes in many forms. One of those forms is a patch that you place on the skin. We speculate that the victim was first sprayed with aerosolized fentanyl, then several patches were placed on her arm to make sure that she slept her way to death. If someone tried to place a patch on your arm, Madison, I presume you would fight them off rather than be compliant?"

"Of course. So, the aerosolized fentanyl made her put her guard down and was a part of the overdose?"

"Yes, in the aerosolized form, the drug would hit you much faster than a patch."

"Wow, how did you guys figure out what happened?"

"It comes down to collecting evidence and trying to re-enact the scene, so we understand how it happened. Sometimes that allows us to eliminate some suspects. With this homicide, the murderer could be anyone from a teenager and up. We hope that a child would be unable to figure out how to aerosolize a drug."

"This is so interesting. You've got to call me to join you on your next case. I'll do it for free just for the experience," Madison said.

"What's your end game, Madison?"

"What do you mean?"

"How will interning with me help you decide what you want to be when you grow up? Are you learning stuff by working with the detectives here?"

"I'm stuck in the office doing computer work for them. I don't get the opportunity to think through a case."

"Actually, most of the work that detectives and PIs do is on a computer. The scene of the crime is interesting and sometimes it tells you something about your suspect, but the majority of investigative work is done away from the crime scene, like what you're doing with this videotape. As we understand this crime scene, the killer is in one of those twenty-three cars in the video. You're doing detective work right now, Madison."

CHAPTER 16

*J*ill and Madison moved to a conference room, where Detective Parnell joined them. Jill had a car service bringing Brenda to the meeting location. Brenda could have continued to do work from their suite, but Jill thought she would have more fun and memories if she joined them at the police station.

"So, what do we have?" The detective asked.

"We checked with three homeowners who had cameras facing the road to the church ruin. With one home, the home-owner said the camera was fake. Its purpose was to deter people from breaking into their property. In the case of the second home, the owners are out of the area for a couple of months and had the system turned off. With the third home, as you know, we struck gold with the homeowner. We copied his tape for the time period in question and brought it back here to analyze. There were twenty-three cars on the road, and we reviewed twenty-one of those twenty-three as the other two cars were simply turning into the homeowner's residence. One other car belonged to homes along that road. We were left with twenty cars to investigate. The picture was clear enough on about half of them for Jill to use her facial identity software. The other half we could at least identify the car's ownership by the license plate." Madison summarized, while Jill looked on with approval.

"So, what did you find?"

"One person had an outstanding warrant for speeding, two other drivers were behind in renewing their vehicle registration — those were the only non-law-abiding citizens on that road. Or perhaps I should say, those three were the ones with records."

"Madison, did you find me any suspects?" The detective asked with a bland expression on his face.

"No, Sir. Not yet. We need to do more research. Jill has someone joining us soon and the three of us will run down these twenty people."

"How about the church? Did your teammate finish her analysis?"

"Yes, on the plane home. She emailed a chart this morning; it's on my laptop," Jill said, sharing the screen with the other occupants of the room.

There was silence as they read the detail in Jo's chart.

"It seems that I need to talk to Elder Williams. Do you think that is the same Williams whose house you got the tape from earlier?"

"Williams is a common name, but if it is and I was a congregation member of this church, I would be concerned given the distance between the church's coffers and the value of Mr. Williams' estate," Jill said. "Even as member contributions have declined, the church has had to spend significant money for the upkeep of their leader's home. In fact, for the previous two years, the church has spent more for upkeep on the home than upkeep for its five physical churches. No wonder Laura Locklear was furious with the management of the church. In times of financial distress, do you improve the home of one or the homes of all?"

"However, is that a motive for murder?" Madison asked.

"You'd be surprised at how often in my cases money is a motive for murder. Once my team member arrives, I'll concentrate on Elder Williams' profile, while Brenda and Madison investigate the drivers. Detective, give me half an hour and I'll give you some information to take with you when you interview Elder Williams."

"Sounds like a plan," the detective said, standing up and planning to leave just as Brenda was escorted in by someone from the reception area.

Like many law-abiding citizens, Brenda had never been inside a police station, and Jill could tell her mother-in-law was in awe. More memories to store and talk about when she returned home.

"Hi Brenda, this is Madison. She's helping us with the search for suspects. Can you share Marie's instructions with her while the two of you search for information on our twenty drivers? I'm going to take a detour for a moment and search for information about a church leader whom the detective needs to interview."

Soon there was no noise in the room other than the faint sound of keyboard keys and pen on paper as information was added about each driver. Jill was frowning in concentration and silently tsking as she worked to uncover information about Elder Williams.

The man they met that morning had been the Williams in question. Now Jill had a whole other feeling about the big house they visited that morning. From what she understood of Jo's report, the land, the house, the fence, the driveway, the security system were all thanks to the parishioners of the Presbyterian churches in the Asheville region. That would stir up a lot of resentment among the parishioners to see their funds spent in that manner. Jo provided a list of five names who repeatedly had concerning thoughts about the church upkeep of Elder Williams' estate. Her friend also included a statement that the church had insufficient funds to pay for this year's maintenance. Judging by what she saw, Elder Williams and his family might be forced out of their beautiful estate later that year if they wanted to keep the church operational.

There were large houses occupied by religious leaders all over the United States. The church considered it a part of religious housing and it was tax-free. Jill wondered what was going on with the church. Was the house a recent purchase? The church had roots dating back over a hundred years, and it seemed unlikely that the estate she'd seen that morning had been owned a hundred years ago as it wasn't geographically close to the church. Asheville would have been a smaller town then, and any church housing would likely be within a mile of the downtown church.

About an hour into the search, Jill was tired of sitting on the conference room chair. She stood up and did a few stretches, interrupting Madison and Brenda's work with her movements.

"Did you find something on Elder Williams?" Madison asked.

"Yes and no. I'm not used to sitting in a chair for long hours, so I needed to stretch. I'm sorry I interrupted your concentration. The stuff I found on Elder Williams disappoints me. The upkeep of his house that we visited this morning is the biggest expenditure of the church. There's something wrong with that and I'm disappointed in my fellow man for allowing this to happen."

"I don't belong to that church, so I don't know who he is or how well he's thought of in this community. Is he a native to Asheville?" Madison asked.

"He is native, but his first wife died about nine years ago and he married another woman about four years ago, and that's when it seems like the house got very expensive."

"Did he live in the house before that?" Brenda asked.

"He did. The house is over a hundred years old and has belonged to the church for a good part of that time. However, the new wife undertook major renovations. It was under the guise of modernizing an old home. An old house does need structural updates, but they've spent over a quarter million dollars of the church's money in the last few years. It's been the biggest administrative expense for the church."

"I would think that any parishioner who is mad about these finances would most likely try to fire him, not kill someone else in the church who also was complaining about finances," Brenda said.

"Detective Parnell is on his way to interview Elder Williams. I'll text him some of this information. I'm sure he's going to ask him for an alibi at the time of Laura's murder. His house is about four miles away from the church ruin, but it's along the road that people would drive to reach the ruin. Someone could have walked the distance there but Laura wasn't the only outspoken parishioner upset with the church finances."

"True, it sounds like a problem for Elder Williams but not enough of a motive for Laura's murder."

"Did the detective say when he was interviewing that other bride and groom to find the name of the woman who disrupted their wedding?" Madison asked.

"He didn't say other than he was going to do it today, so I'm guessing by the time he comes back he will have interviewed Elder Williams and the married couple," Jill said. "Let's go find some lunch and then we'll get back to looking up information."

The three women were finishing their lunch of sandwiches at a local café when both Madison and Jill received a text from the detective saying he had fresh news to share with them. Madison returned the text with the response that their ETA was five minutes. They were soon crossing the road to return to the station and were grateful for Madison's badge, which helped them negotiate the doors at the station. They arrived to find the detective in the conference room writing some notes on the whiteboard.

CHAPTER 17

*A*shley Monroe was a pretty girl at the age of twenty-three. She graduated from college and worked as the marketing person for a furniture company. A year ago, life had looked full of promise. She had her new college degree, a new job, and an apartment in a young area of Asheville. A man she met in college that she thought would be her future husband also moved to Asheville and had his own apartment. He settled into the town and had a job in the marketing department of a large hotel. She expected he would propose any day. She dreamed of a church wedding in a beautiful white wedding gown. She danced around her apartment in secret delight and anticipation of that special day in her future.

She was so caught up in her dream that she didn't notice Brandon pulling away. It took her at least a month to realize he had reduced their time together. When she brought it up to him, he said he'd met someone else who interested him. He didn't know for sure that this new woman would be a better partner for him than Ashley, but he needed to try.

Ashley was dumbfounded. What was Brandon talking about? They were perfect for each other. Then she thought of all of the little signals he'd been giving out. He was busy with work at night, he turned down invitations to dinner at her parents' house . . . By the time she became aware of the situation, he'd grown distant.

With her usual enthusiasm, as she never failed to get what she wanted in the past if she worked hard enough for it, she doubled down on her relationship with Brandon, but that seemed to just push him farther away. Finally, she knew it wasn't her or Brandon it was that other woman. She must have bewitched Brandon. There was no other explanation for it— Brandon stopped going out with Ashley altogether.

Ashley started following Brandon around, determined to find out who the other woman was to break her spell on him. Asheville was a big city, and it took her nearly a month to find this other woman. She began waiting outside his apartment to follow him and was distressed when he didn't show up at his apartment. She was sure he was out of town on business. Then she checked with the hotel and found that he was at work. Was he spending the night at that woman's house? She had to know.

She took a week off work as she needed to follow him around and it was causing her to lose sleep. Finally, she spotted him with his arm around a woman's waist. They stopped at one point and kissed while Ashley moaned in pain. When she opened her eyes, they were gone. They had entered a nearby restaurant. Ashley pondered what to do next. Should she wait and confront the two of them and try to break the woman's spell? Should she try to get rid of the woman? She needed to find out more about her, so her immediate plan was to follow them home. That first night they returned to his apartment and Ashley slept in her car, grateful that no one roused her.

The next morning, she followed Brandon and the other woman as he dropped her off at her home. Ashley waited outside the witch's home to find out where she worked. Sure enough, about an hour later, Ashley had the opportunity to follow the woman to her work. She was disappointed when the woman got out of her car at the same large luxury hotel where Brandon worked. It must be a workplace romance, but Ashley was confident that she could break it off and bring Brandon back to her. She went home to rest and think about her next steps.

Ashley had the rest of the week to follow the woman. She found out her name was Caitlin thanks to a coffee shop calling out her name. *Caitlin* sounded like a witch's name. She spent that first week following Caitlin everywhere except work. She didn't want to get caught stalking the woman before she had an explanation ready, and she didn't have one yet. It never occurred to her that what she was doing was wrong; she just saw herself as freeing Brandon from Caitlin's spell.

She struggled for weeks trying to resolve what to do about Caitlin. All the while she watched while Brandon escorted her everywhere. She was so obsessed with following the couple that she stopped hanging out with friends and couldn't look for a new boyfriend as she was focused on Brandon. He was the perfect man for her; why look elsewhere?

She was outraged when she opened the paper and saw the engagement of Brandon and Caitlin with a wedding date set in a month. That was supposed to be her wedding and her husband. She was consumed by anger and debated killing Caitlin. However, by the time she made her mind up to do that, the wedding day was upon her. Still, she decided to show up at the wedding. When the pastor marrying them asked the audience to *speak now or forever hold your peace*, Ashley would take that moment to object. Yes, that would be her plan.

On the appointed day, Ashley waited in her car until she heard the wedding ceremony start. The wedding was being hosted in a Presbyterian church on the south end of town. Ashley had been in the church before the wedding so she could decide where to sit. She took a seat on the groom's side and seethed with rage at the imposter's position at the altar as she waited to stand and deny the wedding. She listened to the passages read by the pastor and critiqued them. Before she realized it, Brandon and Caitlin were pronounced man and wife.

Before she realized what she was doing, Ashley stood up and said, "You're wrong, you can't pronounce them husband and wife. Where's the passage of speak now or forever hold your peace? You didn't do the whole wedding ceremony."

Everyone was shocked by her announcement. *Good,* she thought, *now everyone will speak up about why this wedding shouldn't take place.* There were murmurs in the church and soon she was surrounded by groomsmen who locked her in place in her pew. The bride and groom walked down the aisle and out of the church with their witnesses following. Ashley looked on in disbelief. Once the church was empty, the groomsmen left her alone with the officiant of the wedding ceremony.

"Hello, I'm Laura Locklear and I officiate at weddings. Nowadays most bridal couples eliminate the phrase, 'speak now or forever hold your peace.' Historically, that phrase dates back hundreds of years when people were unsure if they could legally marry. Brandon and Caitlin satisfied all the legal requirements of this county to be married. Today's ceremony just made it official. What's your name?"

"My name is Ashley and Brandon is supposed to marry me. He's just been influenced by that woman. I was hoping to break her hold on him today, but you never gave me a chance."

"Did Brandon already marry you?" Laura asked, puzzled. She'd had several conversations with the bride and groom before today's ceremony. She'd liked both of them and now she hoped that Brandon wasn't into polygamy.

"We just didn't have our ceremony yet. We met at school and dated for years; we were going to get married."

Laura didn't know what to say. Clearly, the lady had a distorted view of reality. All she could think to say was,

"Brandon legally married Caitlin two days ago. Today's ceremony was for friends and family. I don't know what kind of promises he made to you in the past, but Brandon is not married to you now nor will he be in the future. He's married a different woman."

Ashley felt a stab to her heart and with the officiant's last words she ran out the side door of the church to her car. She drove home trying to think of what she would do next. Her heart was broken as she paced her apartment. A text came in from her mother inviting her to dinner. Ashley wasn't feeling very well and declined the invitation, countering that she would stop by the next evening for dinner. She alternated that night between crying and plotting Caitlin's death. She still had no plan, but after many ice packs throughout the day, she faced her parents for dinner that night.

She arrived early and let herself inside through the side entrance she had always used when living in the house. Starting toward the living room, she heard her parents arguing. That was a rarity. She couldn't remember the last time she heard them raise voices at each other. She stopped to listen, hoping they weren't arguing about her.

"I want to finish remodeling this house. We need to bring it into the twenty-first century," she heard her mother say. *Good,* Ashley thought, they're not talking about me.

"We don't have funds in the church to pay for that at this time," she heard her stepfather say.

"The church owes us a parsonage; they need to pay for the updates."

"Well, that may be, dear, but the church doesn't have the money in the budget. One of my board members is stirring the pot on the church budget. Now, they are all paying attention and they've budgeted only two-thousand dollars for emergency repairs for this year."

"Well, you need to make them change their minds. You have

an important role in the church. They need to take care of your home. They do that for every leader and you're responsible for all seven churches. How can they allow just two thousand for this house?"

"Our church membership has been declining and we lost contributions during the pandemic. Last year we were saved by free government money, but not this year."

"Who has said no to our modernization? I want names, and I'm going to call people myself. They need to understand how old and drafty this house is. Yeah, I know repairs are expensive, but they didn't do any for nearly forty years, and so it seems like a lot, but we're playing catch-up."

"Now dear, not this year. I need to work on increasing membership."

"How can we do that if we don't have a place to entertain our congregation in comfort?" his wife continued. "Who is leading the board against our house repairs? Oh wait, it's Laura Locklear, right? She's in charge of the budget committee. Maybe she's the one denying repairs to this house."

Ashley had heard enough. Yesterday a woman by the name of Laura Locklear had married away the man she loved and her best prospect for a husband. Today a woman by the same name was stopping her mother from making necessary repairs to her home. Something needed to be done about Laura Locklear. She would give some thought to getting Laura out of their lives. She suddenly felt the depression lift from her shoulders. She had a plan to work on. Ashley tiptoed back outside the side door and walked around to the front door making lots of noise, "Mom, Dad, I'm home! What's for dinner?"

CHAPTER 18

"What did you learn from your interviews this morning, Detective?" Jill asked as they sat down in the conference room.

"The bride and groom delayed their honeymoon until this week, even though they were married a month ago. It took me a while to run them down on the Yucatan Peninsula. They were very sad to hear that Laura was murdered. Like you, they said she did a wonderful job officiating their ceremony. The woman who made the commotion at their wedding was Ashley Monroe. The groom had dated her steadily through the last years of college and moved here because of a job opportunity. It also happened to be Ashley's hometown. Meanwhile, he met his bride on the job and delayed telling Ashley that he had found someone else. She finally noticed that he had been distancing himself from her and tried to rekindle the relationship. Unfortunately for Ashley, he admitted he had met someone else.

"He had no idea that he had hurt Ashley's feelings so badly until she made a scene at the wedding. That was the last he saw of her, but he did know that his officiant stayed behind in the church to talk to Ashley. Laura told him later that Ashley was quite distressed and ran out of the church, and that was the last time he heard anything about Ashley or Laura."

"Okay, we'll add her to our suspect list. Have you interviewed her today?"

"I tried to reach her, but I just got voicemail. The groom told me where Ashley worked, so I tried that company, and they told me she was on vacation this week. She was planning a trip to Hawaii with her friends."

"Did you check the airports to see if she left?" Jill asked.

The detective looked at her with raised brows. "Really, Dr. Quint, I expected better of you given your record of accomplishment with the FBI and other law enforcement bodies. You know that I can't pick up the phone and call the airline and ask them if someone had flown out on one of their planes. I must get a subpoena, which I've requested from a judge, but in the best of circumstances, I won't have that information for at least forty-eight hours."

"You're right, Detective. I obtain so much random information about suspects and victims online that I forget there are still things that require a subpoena to obtain. I'll check her social media feed and see if I can find any evidence of her being in Hawaii. My apologies."

The detective nodded, signaling her apology was accepted.

"I also interviewed Elder Williams. He was alone at the time and said his wife was in town. He was most surprised to get a second call from the police department today on a different but related subject. He thought I was going to collect additional video footage from his driveway system. He was surprised when I asked him about Laura Locklear. He described her as a parishioner in good standing with the church. He also described her efforts at teaching the next generation about history and God," the detective said.

· · ·

Jill recited:

"Damn with faint praise, assent with civil leer,
   And, without sneering, teach the rest to sneer;
   Willing to wound, and yet afraid to strike,
   Just hint a fault, and hesitate dislike . . .

"That's from Alexander Pope from many years ago."

The detective smiled. "I'd heard that phrase before, but never so poetically put. Elder Williams definitely damned Laura Locklear with faint praise. He wasn't being sarcastic, just polite and lean with his words. I asked him about an alibi for the time period in question and he has a good one, so I didn't question him about the church's finances as he would be the one with the motive. Have you finished with drivers on the road?"

"We have five more to go. However, nothing about the first fifteen drivers screams 'potential murderer of Laura Locklear.' I'll have Madison and Brenda finish those last five drivers and I'll get to work on Ashley Monroe. Madison, can you pull up the DMV record to see what Ashley Monroe drives?"

The detective watched the three women go back to typing away on computers. He gave them a wave and left the room to do his own research.

"She drives a red Ford Mustang. That doesn't sound like your dark-colored midsize SUV."

"No, it doesn't. However, that fact alone doesn't take her off our suspect list. Let's keep searching."

Nathan had checked in with her to get a sense of her schedule for the day and later to let her know that he would be taking Angela straight to the airport as they'd had a busy day of photography.

Jill dropped an email to Melissa, who would be home in

California by now. She was curious as to whether the criminal psychologist could see Ashley Monroe as the killer, given her odd behavior.

She resumed her search for information about Ashley. She stumbled on a picture on social media, and it took her a moment to make the connection.

"Oh my gosh, I think Elder Williams is Ashley Monroe's stepfather."

She stood up, planning to head to the detective's office, and nearly bumped into him when he made the turn into the conference room. They both spoke at the same time:

"Ashley Monroe's stepfather is Elder Williams."

"Detective, how did you find that information?"

"He's listed as co-owner on the registration for her car. How did you make the connection?"

"There's a picture of her with her parents on social media. She has a different last name, so I assume that he is her stepfather. I'm going to investigate her mother. Madison, when you spoke to Mrs. Williams on the phone this morning, what did you think of that interaction?" Jill asked.

"What do you mean?"

"In that short conversation you had this morning, could you tell if she was intelligent, inpatient, befuddled? What emotions did you hear in her voice?"

Madison paused, playing back the conversation in her mind a few times, and then shook her head. "I would hate to label her as anything at this point; my conversation with her was too short. If anything, I would say she was uninterested in my questions. Given that she was gone when we got there, maybe she was on her way out the door when the phone rang, and so she quickly passed us off to her husband."

"That's fair," Jill said. Jill had years of maturity and experience on Madison, and she knew that she didn't always pay attention to conversations she had with people unless she was suspicious of them.

"I'll take a deep look into this family," the detective said. "It will be interesting to compare notes."

Jill heard the challenge in his voice and smiled at him, saying, "Game on."

Silence resumed in the room for another half-hour until Madison and Brenda finished their research on all the drivers.

"I don't think anything is here. Given people's home addresses, most of these twenty drivers had a good reason to be on the road last Friday. There's one person who appears to be from out of the area, but you all think that Laura knew the person who killed her, and on the surface, there's no reason for this person from out of town to know her," Brenda said.

Jill looked at the time and it was getting to be late afternoon. She and Brenda would do more research that night and then they were all departing mid-day the next day. Madison was watching her, seeming to try and read what was going on in her head.

"I don't think we will solve this case before we leave tomorrow. We'll do some more research tonight and in the morning, and then we'll head home," Jill said. "Darn, I was hoping to solve this case before I left town."

"Yeah, but we eliminated like twenty people from the suspect list and developed a new suspect who appears to be strong," Madison said.

"Yes, but if she was in Hawaii, then she's got a solid alibi and we're left with no strong suspects," Jill said. "We do have a strong piece of evidence that we haven't matched yet. It's the fingerprint on the cellophane that we picked up as evidence. Of course, we don't know if someone randomly threw it out the window or if it belongs to our murderer."

"So, what will you do now?" Brenda asked. She had been so hopeful that they would solve the murder before they left town.

She could see how difficult it was to find a suspect in a case like this. On TV, they wrapped everything up in an hour. It was so much more difficult in real life. At least her daughter-in-law had good contacts in this police department and could work on the case from California.

"I'll continue digging information up on Ashley Monroe tonight and tomorrow morning. I'll see if I can verify where she was at the time of Laura's murder. The fact that she's on vacation this week doesn't mean she wasn't in this area last Friday. She could have flown out on Saturday. Then again, she might not be there at all. Too bad the detective didn't know she was Elder Williams' stepdaughter at the time he interviewed him."

"I'd offer to come to California and help you solve this case, but really, given the kind of work that is needed, we can do it over video chat. Would you leave me your information?" Madison asked.

"Of course. Madison, you should think about the work we did in this room today. We were being different kinds of detectives from Detective Parnell. He has the badge and the authority that goes with it, so it's easier for him to gain interviews with people involved in a case. As a private detective, I don't have that luxury. I can't compel people to talk to me. Fortunately, most people leave a very wide trail all over the Internet and all you have to do is look. Eventually, there may be DNA with this case, and certainly there will be fingerprints to match. If I see the right case come along, and it's inside the United States, and you can get time off from your job here at the police department, I'll give you a call to see if you want to join me. I can't promise to pay you for your time. I take some jobs knowing that I won't get paid for them, like this case. However, if it is a paid case, I'll share the wealth with you."

"Cool. Here's my card with my numbers both at the station and my personal cell phone," Madison said, passing a card to Jill. Jill in turned gave the young woman her card. Over the years, many people had wanted to join Jill's team. Some meant it in jest, while others thought she lived an exciting and exotic life. There was nothing exciting or exotic if you had to leave your home in the very early hours to go perform an autopsy on a dead person. However, she didn't think Madison was cut out for medical school. She was smart enough to go, but you had to do a lot of boring, repetitive work for several years before you were released into your profession. Madison might enjoy being a private detective if she could think on her feet and mix that with solid computer skills. Only time would tell.

"My shift is at an end. I can give you both a ride back to your hotel."

Jill looked at her watch and thought that Nathan was either wrapping up or driving Angela to the airport at the moment, so she accepted Madison's offer. Jill and Brenda stopped by Detective Parnell's office on their way out to the parking lot.

"Detective Parnell, it's been a pleasure to make your acquaintance. I'm going to continue to work on the case from California. I leave here around noon tomorrow, so if something comes up between now and then, please give me a call. Have you gained any information in the last half-hour that I can do anything with tonight?"

"Dr. Quint, this has been my strangest experience on a case since I made detective. Of all the civilians who have suggested they could help me solve a case, you've been the one who actually brought a lot of skills to the table. Thank you and we'll stay in touch."

Jill and Brenda women walked out to the parking lot following slightly behind Madison to her car. It was a late-model German sports car and Jill couldn't help herself.

"Madison, do you have a wealthy father?"

"Yeah."

"You have so much money that you could do anything you

want in the world and you're searching for that right thing, aren't you?"

"Yeah."

"I wouldn't think your father would be happy with you risking your life as a policewoman, a detective, or private detective."

"He's not happy. He thinks working here will be just another job shadow opportunity for me and that I'll give it up and move on to something safer."

"What do you think?"

"I see possibilities. He would give me the seed money to open a private detective agency. He would do that because he loves me, and he thinks it's a temporary whim and I'll eventually come back to the family business."

"What's the family business?"

"You know that big beautiful hotel that you're staying at? My father owns that and a few other hotels of that same elegance around the world."

"Do you have an apartment or cottage on the grounds of the hotel?"

"Yes."

"We're staying in the Bedford suite. If you're not doing anything, swing by at seven tonight and we'll do some more work."

They reached the hotel a short time later and Madison dropped them off under the main entrance awning.

CHAPTER 19

Jill and Brenda headed toward Jill's suite, intent on finding out what the plans were for dinner.

"You were very kind to Madison. That young woman has the world at her feet due to wealth and yet doesn't know what she wants to do."

"It took me a while to figure out her motivation for being an intern. She has intelligence and will; she's just confused by too many choices. I don't believe that forensic pathology is for her, but perhaps private detecting. Too bad I didn't meet her when I had the entire team here. She would have been awed by everyone. She might do well as a private detective. Who knows what the future holds for Madison?"

They walked into the suite to find Nathan and his father in the kitchen discussing dinner.

Jill walked over to Nathan to give him a kiss. "How did your day go? Did you get all the pictures you needed?"

"Angela did a phenomenal job and yes, we have all the camera angles we need. My work is done here and I'm ready to go home."

"It's been an extraordinarily busy week. My sightseeing plan was shot to pieces with the wedding and murder. What time were you planning on eating?"

"Why, are you starving?"

"No. I invited somebody to stop by at 7 o'clock to work on the case."

"I have enough for an extra meal. Why don't you invite them to join us?"

"Okay. It's the daughter of the owner of this resort. Let me text her."

Jill took a moment to do that and looked up to find Nathan staring at her.

"How did you meet the owner's daughter? Not that I know who the owner is or if he or she has a daughter."

"Madison is an interesting person," Brenda said as she shared a glance with Jill.

"There's a story there. Where did you meet Madison?" Nathan asked.

"She's interning as a Police Explorer with the police department and helped us today. She offered us the drive home in her late-model German sports car. That was when I hazarded a guess that her father was rich, as I don't know many early twenty-somethings who drive such vehicles."

"I would think her rich father would not be happy with a police officer as a choice of future occupation."

"She accepted your invitation to dinner and asked to bring a guest. Do you have enough food for six people?"

"We can make that happen. I'll run out and get another chicken breast," Charles said.

Jill nodded and typed something on her phone.

Jill opened the door at close to seven that evening to find an older man standing behind Madison. She made introductions.

"Hi Jill, this is my father, Stephen Lewis."

Jill shook hands with the man and welcomed him inside. "Come meet my husband and his parents." Jill felt a little moment of shock realizing it was the first time she referred to Nathan as her husband.

Introductions were made all around and Nathan said, "We've enjoyed staying at your resort and your concierge was most helpful in helping us locate a wedding venue. He was also helpful when we needed the dry erase board so that Jill could work on the murder of our officiant."

"When my daughter came home from work today and told me who she met and the fact that she wanted to be a private detective, I did a quick search on the guests in our Bedford suite. I now have a bigger picture of the situation. The two of you were here on wine business, and you threw in a last-minute wedding. And then a woman was found dead in the vineyard next to an old church ruin that you were married in. Meanwhile, Jill here is actually Dr. Jill Quint, a relatively famous forensic pathologist, private detective, and solver of crime all over the world. Is my summary correct?"

"You forgot to say that Nathan Conroy is a world-famous wine label artist," Jill said without expression.

"Actually, the summary above was just about you, Dr. Quint."

"Please, it's Jill. You're mad that I've influenced your daughter to be a private detective."

"Yes and no. I'd rather she be a private detective than a cop, but I'm not thrilled with either choice. Still, she may have a purpose and direction, so that's not all bad."

"You are hoping that the private detective thing is a passing fancy, and you could be right. This is such an odd case that we're working on at the moment. A lot of private detective work is really boring and related to divorce work. There's also the problem of convincing law enforcement officers worldwide that you can legitimately help them solve a case."

"I'm standing right here. The two of you are discussing me as though I was in another room."

"Actually, Madison, I was describing the life of a private detective. Because I'm a forensic pathologist and I'm hired to give second opinions on the cause of death, my work will naturally be different from yours. You could of course become a forensic pathologist, but then you have eight years of college education in front of you followed by in-hospital training."

Nathan walked up behind Jill and said, "Dinner will be ready in about ten minutes. Mister Lewis, we don't have a table big enough to seat all of us, but we'll all make do with what we have. I'm serving a stuffed chicken breast, rice pilaf, and mixed fall vegetables with a crisp Chardonnay from a local vineyard that is a new client of mine. I grabbed a pie in town which we'll have a la mode later."

"I didn't mean to barge in on your private dinner party."

"I think you probably did. You wanted to meet the people your daughter worked with earlier today. You're sure to size us all up, but what you see is what you get," Nathan said.

"Did your daughter tell you what work we were doing today?"

"I didn't give her the chance. Why don't you tell me about it now?" Stephen replied.

"Madison, why don't you explain the details of the death of Laura Locklear to your father? I'll add any information you miss."

Madison did as Jill suggested.

"So, your number one suspect is Ashley Monroe. Have you been able to track the fentanyl to her? I've never used any opioids, but I suppose if I needed to I would go to my doctor and complain about back pain. Would that get me the prescription I need?" Stephen asked.

"That approach likely wouldn't work, because most surely your physician would give you other painkillers first, or they would give you the drug in pill form. A patch is more likely to be used by someone with terminal cancer or another painful condition. It's not the drug form that physicians prescribe first when you go to their office to complain about back pain."

"Could I fly to Mexico and get a fentanyl prescription from a pharmacy there?"

"Good question. I haven't been to Mexico that often to understand the pharmacies there, but I'll add it to our list to review. The fact that you've been sucked into asking questions about this case shows you the attraction that your daughter has for this occupation."

"I do see the attraction. My question, Madison, is what happens when you have a boring case? As Jill here said, you may end up doing a lot of boring surveillance to document cheating spouses. Is that how you want to fill your day?"

"You also have to get a license, and that requires some further education," Jill added.

"I'd love to open my own private detective agency and do consulting work for you, Jill, when you get an interesting case. That would keep my skills sharp."

Nathan rearranged the furniture so that he and Jill were seated at the kitchen counter on barstools while Nathan's parents, and Madison and her father sat at the dining table. Nathan and Jill thanked Stephen for having the river float and the golf course available to her wedding party. They also complimented him on the concierge that suggested the ruin. They finished the delicious meal and then Jill returned to the case.

"Brenda, Madison, and I are going to work on the case. Since you operate a winery as part of this resort, Stephen, you may want to join Nathan and Charles and talk wine."

He smiled at his dismissal and joined the other two men for a robust discussion on wine labels and marketing.

"Ladies, how do we rule out Ashley Monroe as our killer?" Jill asked

"Let's find an alibi for her," Madison suggested.

"How?" Brenda asked.

"Let's look at all her social media feeds to see if we can verify that she was in Hawaii. I think you started on that, Jill, but you were unable to find the right evidence. Did you look at Instagram or Tic Tok?"

"No, I started with Facebook."

"My generation doesn't have much time for Facebook; we like Instagram and Tik-Tok better. I'll start with Instagram."

"Since you're the IT whiz, can you tell if any of the pictures she posts are taken that day or sometime in the past?"

"Usually, I can look at the code and tell the origin of the picture, but if she is sophisticated with computers, she would know how to hide that," Madison said.

"Is there a way to tell if she was on a plane or booked a rental car or a hotel in Hawaii?" Brenda asked.

"Not that I'm aware of. How about you, Madison?" Jill said.

"As the detective said, we would need a subpoena for most of that information unless we could trick it out of one of the car companies or hotels, but that could be like looking for a needle in a haystack. There are a lot of hotels and rental car companies, and if we were to fake our way through it, we would at least need to be correct on the arrival and departure dates. I think our best bet is social media."

"Are we asking the wrong question?" Brenda asked. "We know she's on vacation this week, but was she at work last Friday? Sometimes you'll take a Friday off in order to extend their vacation, but usually people leave on a Friday night or Saturday morning and head out somewhere for the week."

"I know someone who works at the furniture company. It's a pretty large company, so they may not know everyone, but let me see if they remember seeing her around or if they know where she was last Friday," Madison said. She picked up her cell phone and her thumbs flew over the phone typing out a message to someone.

Jill and Brenda returned to searching Twitter and Facebook for Ashley's profile. They found her on both social media sites, but she rarely posted or commented, proof that Madison was correct regarding her comments about Facebook; they hoped they would have greater success with Instagram and Tik-Tok.

Nathan broke into the conversation with word that it was time for dessert. He heated up a locally baked apple pie and served it with vanilla bean ice cream. Madison and her father left a short time later to return to their respective residences on the grounds of the resort.

Brenda, who had a mind-boggling day inside of the police station, was ready to hit the sack and gave the eye to Charles that was time to return to their own hotel room.

Jill and Nathan enjoyed the first silence of the day. She went over to hug him and asked, "Did you pick up a new client tonight?"

She felt his chest move underneath her face as he chuckled. "Are you worried that I won't be able to pay my share of your mortgage payment?"

"No, I know you're good for that. I just wondered about your charisma in influencing one of the old influential families of the East Coast."

"I got the job, just not for this site. Stephen has another hotel in Arizona. It's north of Phoenix, closer to Sedona. The contract with the artist for this site is controlled by his brother."

"Somehow, I didn't know they grew wine in Arizona. The grapes like the heat, but not the dry air of the desert."

"I'm in the same boat as you. This will be my first client in Arizona, and I'm going to do some research on the grape industry in that state. Stephen says there are more than a hundred and twenty wineries. I wonder what the percentage of grapes grown on the property versus wine juice is part of the production recipe for those wineries."

They soon made their way to bed, planning on packing in the morning for the flight home. It was the middle of the night when Jill woke up to a siren and flashing lights. She got out of bed and went to look out the suite windows. Her cell phone rang, and the caller ID said it was Madison.

CHAPTER 20

"Hi, Madison. What's happening?"

"I'm here with the fire department and my father. Someone just tried to burn my house down with me inside of it."

"Can you have someone pick me up in a golf cart and bring you over to your house? I don't know where you live on the estate."

"You'll need to drive here. Most of the hotel staff are tied up dealing with the emergency vehicles and calls that are being made to the front desk. Do you have a pen and paper? I'll read you my GPS coordinates."

"Go ahead"

Ten minutes later, Jill and Nathan arrived on the edge of many flashing lights. They parked in a place they hoped would not obstruct the departure of any of the emergency vehicles. They had both thrown on heavy jackets over sweats. They made their way to the house and looked around for Madison.

She was standing next to her father and a person from the fire department. Jill and Nathan hurried over to the group.

"Are you okay, Madison? Do you have any burns? Did you inhale any smoke?"

"I forgot you're a doctor. I managed to get out without smoke or burns. Thank you for coming. This is Chief Brown from the Asheville Fire Department."

"Was an accelerant used?"

"Ma'am, what do you know about accelerants?" the fire chief asked her with suspicion.

"Chief Brown, I'm Dr. Jill Quint, a forensic pathologist working on a murder case with Madison here. I'm also a private detective, and in my last case, we caught a serial wildfire killer in California. That killer used an accelerant to start the fires. Is that what happened here?"

"Yes, ma'am. When we got here, we could smell gasoline. Our arson investigator will be here soon to give us an official report, as will detectives from the police department. This is an attempted murder scene."

"Were your doors blocking you inside the house?" Jill asked.

"Yes. Boards were slid through the latch on the front and back doors so the doors would not open. The killer didn't know that this house has a root cellar. I ran down the basement stairs and then up through the root cellar steps on the side of the house. I called 9-1-1- and then Dad."

"That was really good thinking on your part, Madison. I'm glad you didn't panic. Instead, you turned your considerable brain to help you get out of this situation. Did you see anyone driving away or running away from your house?"

"No. There's so much land and forest around my house that it would be easy for someone to melt away."

"They couldn't have parked too far away. It's not easy to carry a couple of gallons of gas through the woods in the dark. I suspect come daylight there will be some tracks to follow. I wonder why you were attacked. Who even knows you're working on this case?"

"Just the police department knows that it's part of my assignment."

"And Mr. Williams and the people you spoke to who have cameras on the road to the church ruin."

"Yes." Madison looked over Jill's shoulder to see a rumpled Detective Parnell rushing toward Madison.

"Chief, Dr. Quint, Mr. Conroy, and you Sir—are you Madison's father?"

"Yes, I'm Stephen Lewis. I also own this resort including the house my daughter nearly died in."

"Mr. Lewis, I'm Detective Parnell from the Asheville Police Department," he said, holding up his badge for identification. "Your daughter has done some work for me on various issues around the police department. I'm glad that she's safe." He looked Madison over and asked the same questions Jill had, "Were you injured, Madison? Do you have burns or smoke inhalation that needs treatment?"

"No, I'm fine, thank you, Detective. Someone tried to kill me tonight. Will you be the detective assigned to the case?"

"Yes. I'm going to interview each of you, but first I'd like to walk the scene with Chief Brown. Can you find something else to talk about in my absence other than this fire?"

They nodded and the detective walked off with the fire chief. Several trucks were putting away their gear and getting ready to leave the scene. An ambulance arrived with the fire department but left when they found no one needing their services at the site.

Jill had discussed the situation with Nathan on the short drive to Madison's house and said, "Nathan and I discussed the ramifications of someone trying to kill you. I presume you don't have an ex-boyfriend who is an arsonist?"

Madison looked embarrassed at the question, but she shook her head "no."

"In prior cases, I've become the target of a killer who thinks that if they eliminate me the investigation will go away. That's faulty thinking on the part of the criminal. Stephen, if your hotel can make room for us, we would like to extend our stay here for a few days."

"My daughter is everything to me. I would've asked you to stay if you hadn't volunteered to do so. I've already taken care of your hotel room and I've comped the full stay. Find my daughter's attempted killer."

"Thank you. I appreciate your help with our hotel arrangements. Madison, it looks like there's some damage to your house, and you should not stay there tonight, or what remains of the night. Are you moving in with your father? Never mind that question. Stephen, you should ask your security staff where Madison would be safest and put her there."

"I already asked them that question, and she's been moved to the suite near yours. We have many more security cameras in the main lodge. It will be much harder to get to her there."

Jill opened her mouth to say something more, but then closed it again remembering her promise to the detective. Instead, she said, "When the fire chief gives the all-clear, you'll probably want to go inside and pack a few items for your move to the main hotel."

The group stood in an awkward silence looking at the activity around them, each of them with their own thoughts and questions. They stayed that way until the detective returned with the fire chief.

"Madison, I'd like to interview you first. Would you step away with me while I take your statement?" She nodded, and the two of them moved out of hearing range of the larger group.

"I'm not one to lecture, but if you do a Google search on our friend Dr. Jill Quint, she's been the target of many a murderer in her past cases. That's a danger to you if you follow her footsteps and become a private detective. For some reason, criminals go after non-cops at a greater rate than bona fide law enforcement officers. Just a few thoughts to help you make up your mind about your career. Now let's recount what happened here. What woke you up?"

"I heard a noise on the edge of my consciousness. I think it was the sound of fire. As I was trying to identify what sound I thought woke me up, my smoke alarm kicked in and there's no sleeping through one of those. I grabbed a robe, my cell phone, and shoes and ran to the front door. I tried to open it checking the locks, but I couldn't make it budge. Then I ran to the back door and tried the same thing with the same result."

"Did you turn the lights on?"

"I tried but they didn't work. So, I used the light on my cell phone. My house is old and there's a basement beneath it. That basement has a root cellar with steps to the outside. So I ran down to it and up the steps and fortunately outside. I called 9-1-1 once I made it outside. I called my father as soon as I hung up with the emergency operator. Once he arrived, I called Dr. Quint soon after."

"Did you see anyone when you exited your house? I know it was dark and smoky, but the arsonist would have needed a flashlight to walk off the grounds. Can you recall seeing a light as you waited by yourself for help?"

Madison thought back to those tense moments shortly after she had made it out of her burning house. Had she seen a flashlight in the distance? She looked around her house and tried to remember what she saw. It was difficult due to the emergency lights. She always avoided strobe lights as they brought on a headache.

"I think I saw a light over there," she said, pointing to the woods to the left of her house.

"We'll search that area once daylight arrives. You did really well in an emergency situation. You didn't panic. You grabbed your cell phone and you protected yourself. Those are the makings of a good cop if you decide to pursue that field. Did I forget to ask you any questions?"

"No, sir. That sums up my night."

"You'll be released from this scene soon. I'll let the department know that you'll be in the field today and you can help the crime scene team search this area once daylight arrives."

"Thank you. Jill indicated she and her husband are staying a few extra days to work on this case. If they hadn't volunteered, I think my father would have hired her. She has a great reputation."

"Yes, she does. I'm done with your statement. Would you send your father over here next?"

Madison nodded and returned to the group, sending her father over to the detective.

"So, has someone ever tried to light your house on fire?" Madison asked Jill, thinking about the comments the detective made.

"Yes. I've had some criminals throw Molotov cocktails at it, shoot at me, kidnap me, try to paralyze me with a dart gun, and many more awful attempts on my life. When I was Down Under, there were jellyfish swarms, snakes, and spiders. The life of a private detective is not for the faint of heart. You might be safer as a cop, although the risk there is that your average nut case could wreck your day."

"So, what will you do first this morning?"

"Come daylight, I would search for the entrance and exit of your arsonist. The crime scene team should be here and maybe you and I can be extra manpower for them as they conduct the official search."

"And then?"

"I would go to this hotel's security cameras and see where all the cameras are aimed. I would need a map to understand the access points around this resort. Is there a camera on some road that leads away from the resort? That might contain a clue as to who drove here with a gas can."

Stephen Lewis had returned from his interview with the detective and was listening to their conversation and said, "I'll ask the security team to work on that right now. Jill, the detective wants to interview you and Nathan now."

They nodded and walked over to the detective. "I don't think we'll have much to offer on this scene as we arrived well after the fire department and hotel staff.'

"I agree. I wanted to brainstorm with you. Who do you suspect as starting this fire?"

"I'm really prejudiced about this as I have been attacked so many times by the criminals involved in my cases. I asked her if she had an old boyfriend that she angered and she said no. If the arson is related to this case, then there are two sources—Mr. and Mrs. Williams or a leak from your department. She came on the case today and those are the only people who know that she was connected to this case. How long has she been an Explorer in your department?"

"She started about five months ago and is well-regarded. She's smart and friendly. She drives a fancy car, but no one appears jealous of her background."

"Did you know her background?

"I knew she came from a wealthy family, but I didn't realize which wealthy family. So Elder Williams and his wife are at the top of your list of suspects?"

"Yes. My team interviewed other people connected to this case and no one tried to light our suite on fire."

"Yet," Nathan murmured.

"Sadly, you're right about that," Jill agreed.

"I'd like Madison to stay here and work on the case come daylight. The main lodge is busy and has lots of security. She is safer there rather than out on the road or crossing the street into our police department. This was a brazen effort to end her life."

Jill only then realized that the detective was seething inside at an attack on his department. Madison was a part of the blue brotherhood and they stood with her.

"You could assign police protection to her."

"I think her father has taken care of that, and he likely doesn't want a police presence interfering with the ambiance of the resort."

"True. She's level-headed. She asked me what to do to find out who tried to burn her up in her house. If you'll have your crime-scene folks call us when they arrive at daylight, we'll help look for evidence. Mr. Lewis has his security personnel studying the cameras around the grounds to see if they can spot a vehicle from any camera angle."

"So, while I was inspecting the crime site, you were directing how the case was going to be solved?"

"No, Madison asked what I would advise as to next steps to investigate the destruction of her home, and I answered her question. Shouldn't you want that behavior in a future cop?"

The detective rubbed his face and sighed. "It's two in the morning and you're thinking better than I. Just forget I asked that last question. I know you're not directing the investigation. I'm just dreading the politics of one of Asheville's most prom-inent citizens' daughter being the center of an attempted murder investigation. It's going to be an ugly day ahead. The police brass will be out in force crawling all over me to solve this case yesterday."

"I get it, Detective. No worries. I'm here to help not hinder your investigation. We'll take directions very well from your crime scene staff and won't do anything stupid that screws the case up for you."

"Thank you."

The three of them walked over to where Madison and her father were standing.

"The fire chief said they'll be here another hour and then back at daylight. You're free to return to the main lodge and get whatever is left of this night's sleep."

"Madison, do you want a ride to the lodge, or is your father accompanying you?"

"My father is taking me there, as he has some business to conduct there. I'll see you in the morning."

"Okay. Madison, you did well tonight. See you in a few hours."

"Thanks, that means a lot coming from you."

Jill and Nathan made the short drive to return to the main lodge.

"That was a nice gift from Madison's father," Nathan commented.

"It never hurts to make friends in high places. People pass through our lives and I have this Ouija board in my head that suggests whether I'll cross paths with them again. The board suggests we'll cross paths with the Lewis family again."

"Even for you, that is plain weird. I'll chalk that up to our being awake in the middle of the night. By the light of day, all thoughts of Ouija boards will be gone, I'm sure."

"Aren't we the couple—morning zombies and Ouija boards? By the way, did you alert your parents? It sounded like half the hotel heard the commotion, from what Stephen said."

"I texted them, as I didn't want to wake them up if they managed to sleep through the noise. Would it bother you if they decide to stay longer?"

"Not at all. Your mom can help us search for evidence in the morning. Can you imagine the stories she'll have to tell her friends when she returns from her son's wedding? Each day brings her new materials. I don't mean that in a snarky way, but

I'm sure she'll have the weirdest stories to tell among any of her friends."

"I know. Even my father is enjoying his time here. My parents always have this vibe that the wine business is on the level of sophistication that they don't understand. Then you're doing autopsies and investigating deaths—it just blows his mind. They knew what we both do for a living but didn't comprehend it. We've provided them a glimpse into our world and we're like a freeway crash. You don't want to look, but you do anyway."

"That's not a good start to our marriage if you're going to call it a car crash."

"It's not our marriage that's a car crash; it's the way weird cases morph out from our jobs," Nathan said, shaking his head. "I'm getting close to my zombie zone so I may not be making sense."

"I, on the other hand, can feel my brain revving up to the puzzle of these two cases. I'm not sure I'll be able to drop off to sleep."

"I'll work on that for you," Nathan said with a smile as they entered the suite.

CHAPTER 21

Ashley heard through church gossip about the couple who had walked into the church looking for an officiant and ended up with Laura Locklear. She immediately knew she was going to plan something and asked for the week off work starting the Friday of the wedding. She was bingeing on a television series when she got an idea about how to kill Laura so that she could never again marry the wrong people.

Ashley just needed to get her hands on some fentanyl. She thought her mother might have gotten fentanyl to help her recover from surgery last year. Her other choice was to figure out how to buy it on the street. First, she would raid her parents' medicine cabinets when she knew they were out of the house.

A search one day yielded a box of patches. She followed some instructions she saw on the internet on how to make a spray to incapacitate Laura. Everything worked perfectly. She made a spray and tried it on herself one evening and awoke hours later. She was pleased with the results.

She nosed around for information about the wedding and planned her attack on Laura. She estimated when the officiant would leave the ceremony, and then waited outside of the ruin for Laura to make an early exit.

"Hello, Mrs. Locklear, I heard you were officiating at this wedding and since it's close to my parents' house, I thought I would see if you had a few minutes to chat with me before you return to the city."

Ashley could tell the woman was puzzled, but she nodded in agreement.

"Why don't we take a walk to the vineyard, so we won't be interrupted by anyone looking for the porta-potties?" Again, Laura nodded and followed Ashley into the vineyard.

Ashley stopped suddenly, slipped on a surgical mask, and sprayed fentanyl at Laura's face several times. The woman collapsed to the dirt of the vineyard row and Ashley took the opportunity to place patches on Laura's arm. She knelt in the dirt and watched Laura's breathing slow, then stop. She took her pulse and found none. She waited a minute and repeated it. Still no pulse. She removed the fentanyl patches from Laura's body and made a hurried escape to her car parked along the side of the road.

She was quite pleased with herself. Now Laura would no longer preside over any more weddings that shouldn't take place.

She drove the few miles to her parents' house and went inside. Her mother was there, but her stepfather was in town at one of his churches.

"Hey Mom, I got a last-minute deal to take a vacation to Hawaii. I'm leaving in the morning. I won't be around for a week. I have some friends from work who are coming with me."

"That's really great, honey. I haven't been there. Make sure you pack some sunblock as I hear the sun is intense. But why are you driving a strange car?" her mother asked, looking out at the front where Ashley was parked.

"My car is at the dealership for routine maintenance, and this is the loaner car."

"Oh, that is good, dear, that they gave you a loaner. How is it going otherwise?"

"How can I complain? I'm heading out on vacation tomorrow."

"Who are you dating at the moment? We haven't seen Brandon for a while, so I presume you've moved on?"

"Oh, Mom, leave me alone on that," Ashley said with an edge in her voice.

Her mom looked at her more closely, knowing her child very well, "What's up? What have you done?"

Thirty minutes ago, Ashley had been high on her ingenuity. She'd thought of a great way to kill Laura. Now some other part of her mind was screaming, *Tell her what you did*. She put her hands to her head to end the confusion, but then burst out as if in pain, "I just killed Laura Locklear."

Ashley's eyes were closed when she uttered those words, and in the silence of the room, she finally opened her eyes and looked at her mother.

Her mother was staring at her with a confused look on her face. "Did I hear you correctly? You KILLED Laura Locklear? Why?" her mother asked.

"Laura Locklear married Brandon to another woman. Then I heard you and father arguing one afternoon. It seems you wanted to make repairs on this house, and she was leading the church board against you. Our family had two reasons to hate Laura, so I worked on a plan to get rid of her."

"What did you do?" her mother asked, wondering where she went wrong in raising her only daughter. Did she own a gun? Had she killed the woman with a knife? There was no blood on Ashley, so that was a good thing.

"I stole the fentanyl patches from your bathroom and over-dosed Laura with them."

"Did you leave the patches behind?"

"No, I got the idea from a TV show. It will just look like Laura died of a fentanyl overdose."

"Well, at least you were smart about that. I'll figure out what to do. You head for Hawaii tomorrow with your friends, but I warn you—you went too far with Laura: this is the last time I clean up one of your messes."

Ashley glanced down and nodded, "Yes, mother." Her mother soon heard the front door open and close after her daughter left. She had to give kudos to her daughter for thinking of a way to make Laura's death look like an accident. It should work, but she'd keep a close eye on the investigation. She didn't think Ashley would do well if the police questioned her, so better that she be in another state. She had no intention of telling her husband about Ashley's actions. It would be their little secret. She also smiled in hopes that she would get to do her remodeling without Laura around to object to the budget.

Ashley left the next day as planned and all seemed quiet regarding Laura's death. There was much discussion at the church about the loss of Laura, but no trails led to Ashley. Her mom put it out of her mind until she received a call from the police department. They wanted a copy of the driveway camera video feed. She was so flustered that she passed the phone over to her husband and then said she had to go run errands. Instead, she parked farther down the road from the police station and waited for the car to return to the city. She needed to find out who this Police Explorer was and do something about her. She followed the car's occupants into the station and heard someone call out to the girl, "Hey, Madison." She looked to be a year or two younger than Ashley. With a little more sleuthing, she learned that her last name was Lewis and she lived in a cottage on the resort estate at the edge of town.

What should she do about the girl? Surely, she worked for one of the detectives. Maybe she needed to make an attack on her life. If she succeeded, oh well. If she failed, she could do it anonymously and that would take the detective's focus off her daughter and her relationship with Laura.

She studied a map of the resort, particularly, near the cottage area and decided it would be easy to burn it down. She could park on the road in the middle of the night tonight and hike with two one-gallon gas cans. Then she would try to block the doors and torch the place. She liked the idea. Her only question was how to leave her husband's bed in the middle of the night. Given the short notice, she decided she would just drug her husband to make sure he stayed asleep while she was gone. She had her plan and stopped for supplies on the way home. That evening she followed through on her plan. After she doused the cottage and flung a match at it, she then understood the primal satisfaction of eliminating the enemy that her daughter had felt with Laura's death.

CHAPTER 22

*J*ill woke up after less than four hours of sleep. It wasn't in her nature to be tired first thing in the morning, but she knew she would sag in the afternoon.

Charles and Brenda had the opportunity to read Nathan's text the night before. Brenda had heard the sirens, but Charles had slept through it. She was pleased to hear that Madison got out safely. She would be over shortly, and they would also extend their stay by a few days. Charles was enjoying the time with his son, and she was enjoying the case. The fact that she would get to work with a real crime scene team was the icing on the cake.

Madison texted her to see if she was awake and Jill invited her over too.

She opened the door to Nathan's parents, Madison, and her father.

"I ordered room service, but I see I under-ordered; let me correct that," Jill said.

"No worries, I'll make the call," Stephen said, pulling his phone out. He was dressed casually this morning and Jill guessed it was because he would be assessing his daughter's house for repair and possibly joining them on the hunt for evidence.

"How are you feeling this morning, Madison? No burns or smoke in your lungs?" Brenda asked.

"Other than being tired, I'm okay—thank you for asking. Did you hear the full story of what happened?"

"Nathan texted us that there was a fire at your house, and they were staying on to investigate it. Nathan's father and I are staying additional days as well so we can help, no matter our minimal contribution."

"Mrs. Conroy, you been helpful in ways you can't know about. These past twenty-four hours have taught me a lot and given my father's and my ideas for the future, and you've played a role in that."

"Goodness!" Brenda said, her face pink.

"Let me tell you the full story of what happened last night."

Jill was impressed with Madison's description. She did a great job of relaying just the facts. She was excited about searching the woods for evidence and was asking Jill questions of what they should expect and what they should search for. Jill recounted their search of the winery and the road and the evidence that Angela found.

"Search with gloves on and have bags to put your findings in, and tiny flags to mark anything you find as evidence. Don't just look at the ground. A tree branch may catch hair or fiber. I'm sure the crime scene folks will give us instructions. They probably won't be happy that we're there, but be a professional— keep your gloves on and mark where you find evidence."

Madison nodded and then Stephen opened the door to the additional room service. "Let's all grab a bite to eat before we head out. My security team has welcomed the police onto the grounds."

Jill wondered what Stephen was up to. Madison had an

excitement about her that could have come from surviving the fire last night, but Jill thought there was something else. They finished their breakfast and headed outside to a golf cart. Stephen drove them to Madison's house and Jill and Brenda toured a part of the extensive resort grounds that were new to them.

They arrived just after sunrise which was fortunately later in October, and they could see the damage from the fire. The arsonist must have run out of gas as three sides were burned and a fourth was relatively untouched. The house had white siding and looked like it might contain three or four bedrooms. They could see a partially charred board shoved through the latch of the front door. People with the words *fire* and *CSI* on their jackets were walking around the grounds.

Jill didn't have a sense of the geography of the area and so pulled out her phone's map app to understand where the arsonist might have come from.

"Hey guys, come look at this map. I think the arsonist would have parked about here and walked through the forest about here," Jill said, pointing to different spots on her map. "What do you think?"

Madison and Brenda huddled around Jill's phone and looked from it to the surrounding land.

"It makes the most sense. Those gasoline cans would have been heavy and that's the closest public road to park a car," Madison said.

"Okay, I assume your father is handling issues with your house. Let's go introduce ourselves to the CSI team."

The three women walked over to the first CSI person they saw. "Hi, Detective Parnell said we could assist your team in searching for evidence. I'm Jill, and this is Brenda and Madison. That's Madison's house," Jill said, pointing to the fire-damaged cottage.

"You'll need to talk to Jenny. She's our supervisor," the technician said, pointing to someone pulling supplies out of a van.

They walked toward the woman and Jill called out, "Jenny, we're here to help with the search. I'm Jill, and this is Brenda and Madison. Madison is an intern in your department."

"Have you done an evidence search in the past?"

"I have many times. I'm a forensic pathologist, so I know how to safeguard evidence. These two are newbies, but I told them that we would wear gloves, have bags to collect evidence, and use markers to show where we found the evidence."

"I think I'll assign you the forest. If you see anything, don't touch it. Just mark it and come fetch me. Got it?"

Jill made a note to herself to remind Madison that if she decided to become a private investigator, she should expect only marginal cooperation from the police.

Jill nodded and the three of them put gloves on and carried markers. They approached the woods, which were slightly less dense than normal as it was October and leaves had begun to fall. Jill looked back at the house and then at the woods in front of them.

"Let's enter the forest here and spread out so that we're about three to four feet apart and walk toward the road. Remember to look at where you're walking and to pause and look around you for something caught on a tree branch. If you can, avoid stepping in the center of the path. Our arsonist entered the forest at night with a flashlight, so he or she might have entered and exited on different paths. So, look forward and backward as you search."

Jenny said behind her, "Those are excellent instructions. You're better than I thought you were going to be. As you can imagine, I wasn't thrilled when I received the message that civilians were going to help."

"My last case in California was a serial killer and arsonist. I searched at least four wildfire areas after single males were found dead. I don't have your training, but I have plenty of experience."

"Was he convicted?"

"She is awaiting trial at the moment."

"Can you leave me details of that case? I'd like to read up on it."

"Will do."

The three women began their search. Madison placed a marker by a footprint in a damp area. She looked around the footprint and found hair and potentially blood on a small branch. Jenny came over with a toolbox, plaster-casted the footprint, sprayed luminol on the branch and sampled it, and used tweezers to collect the hair.

"Do you think this is some evidence left behind by the arsonist?" Madison asked.

"The footprint is probably your arsonist, as it is fresh. The hair and blood could be from an animal, or it may be human. Given the height of where we found it, it's likely human, though there are black bears in this area," Jenny said. She held the hair sample up to the light and smiled. "This hair is dyed, so unless we have bears raiding our local stores for hair dye, my guess is that this is human hair."

Jill could tell that Madison was relishing her participation in the search, while Brenda was quiet and absorbing things like a sponge.

They searched for a while longer and Brenda found a second footprint. Then they searched the road where the arsonist's car was likely parked. They found no evidence there other than a slightly used tissue. Jenny bagged it, but proving it fell out of a car would be a difficult task. The CSIs collected other evidence around the house's exterior and then Madison was allowed inside to collect her belongings. Her house would be repaired, but she needed to be out of it for two months or so, according to her father. She would stay at the main lodge until the arsonist was caught and then would return to her father's house.

CHAPTER 23

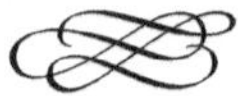

When Jill and Brenda returned to their hotel suite, there was an email message waiting for them from Marie. She had researched Elder Williams and his family in great detail. Marie was confident that Ashley was in Hawaii, having arrived Saturday with some friends.

"That arrival time means she is near the top of our suspect list as she was still here at the time of Laura's murder," Jill said to Brenda. Nathan and his father had managed to snag a tee time. Jill appreciated that Nathan had made plans to enjoy the day without her losing her focus on the case.

"So what are our next steps?" Brenda asked. "How do you decide what to do when you don't work for the police?"

"The police must worry about satisfying the justice system requirements. My goal is to find the one true suspect in the case, and then I leave that in the hands of law enforcement. It's a strategy that has worked worldwide. As to this case, let's read Marie's email, and then we may have to sit back and give the CSIs time to process some of the evidence."

Jill opened Marie's email and shared it with her mother-in-law.

"I asked her to research Elder Williams and his family. Something is going on there. Marie assesses people in her day job. She fact-checks their resumes and then sees what they put on social media. She does the same thing for our cases. She's performed this task hundreds of times, so she is fast and her assessment is usually dead on.

"Marie says that Elder Williams has been with the church for twenty-five years working his way to the top position from when he started out as a theology graduate. He was married to his first wife for fifteen years. They had no children and she died of cancer after a seven-year battle. He married his second wife five years later and became a stepfather to Ashley Monroe. Once he had become the Elder for the regional Presbyterian churches, the house that he currently lives in became his pastoral residence. The previous Elder had died, and the house was empty before the church board appointed Williams as Elder. He lived in the house for perhaps a year with the first wife before she died.

"He married the second wife, a widow, and she demanded funds to redo their bedroom as she didn't want to sleep in the room of his former wife's ghost—this is gossip that was posted about Mrs. Williams as she is not well-liked by her husband's religious community. Apparently, she enjoyed refurbishing the bedroom so much that she demanded other parts of the house be updated. The house is owned by the church, and he's paid a lower stipend as the church takes care of the house. Mrs. Williams doesn't work and so their only source of income is his salary which doesn't support remodeling. The church board approved house updates as it is an old house, but limited the amount last year and completely denied the budget item this year. The parish is declining in numbers and collections, and they lack funds to pay for further house updates."

"So there's friction between the vicar's wife and his parish,"

Brenda summed up the email so far. "That's never a good situation."

"No, it's not. Ashley must have moved into that house when she was in high school and then she graduated from UNC-Charlotte where she got a degree in marketing. After graduation a few months ago, she returned to this area and got a marketing job with a furniture manufacturer, and shortly thereafter moved into her own apartment. There's no mention of whether she was active in her stepfather's church, so she probably wasn't."

"A church Elder marries a woman with a teenage daughter, and they are not active in his church? That seems like a bad decision was made by one of the parties in the marriage. That also would be viewed poorly by the church board that approves the budget. If Mrs. Williams is contributing little to the church, why would they approve her request for more house renovations?"

"Yes, that's a good analysis of Mrs. Williams, Brenda. Marie goes on to say that there are many pictures of Ashley and Brandon at school and in the first month after they returned here, then it drops off the next month, and then there are no more pictures or posts about Brandon or any other guy. So, the relationship came to an end, and nothing replaced it."

"Sounds like both women have something to be angry about, but where is Laura's role in this story? Why would they take their anger out on her? Didn't you say that you look for a motive for each suspect?"

Jill gave her mother-in-law a quick hug and said, "I do look for a motive. Thanks for listening to all the boring details of a case."

"Are you kidding? I have material to discuss with my group of girlfriends when I return home. I'm now going to be their resident expert on all matters criminal. Besides, you've opened my eyes to the human behavior around me. I'll be criticizing mystery shows for the next several years. Maybe the next time Charles and I visit your home in California, you'll have another case I can get involved in as a refresher course. Not that I'm making fun of Laura's death—I'm not. She did a lovely job at your wedding. You've opened my eyes to the people around me and their possible motives for criminal behavior."

Jill shared a smile with her mother-in-law and then said, "Let's go back to Marie's email. She says that Laura served on the budget committee for the church. She was known for running budget questions by her husband, the accountant, and then quoting his advice in the meeting. That lent more power to her statements. Mr. Williams likely would have relayed to his wife about who was speaking out against their renovation budget item. Marie's assessment is that despite his leadership role in the church, he was a weak man as evidenced by his willingness to marry a woman who didn't support his faith to the degree he should expect as a church Elder. Marie speculates that it was easier to blame Laura than tell his wife that her renovation request exhibited poor judgment considering the church's finances."

"So there's our motive; two women in one family upset with Laura Locklear for different reasons."

"Exactly."

"What's your next step?"

"I'll call the detective and discuss Marie's research and assessment. Then we wait for evidence findings. Do you want to head into town and try a restaurant?" Jill asked.

CHAPTER 24

Jill and Nathan enjoyed the Asheville area longer than they wanted. It was nearly two additional days before the test results from the fire arrived. In the interim, she got to know her in-laws better. She could see traits of Nathan in them.

Jill looked at her phone and said, "Finally!"

"Did the results arrive?" Brenda asked.

"They did indeed. The detective has scheduled a meeting in our suite in thirty minutes. As enjoyable as this golf game has been, I'd much rather talk to the detective."

"Hey, we're not bad company!" her father-in-law protested.

"No, but my wife always prefers talking about a murder to the exclusion of almost anything else."

"Ha ha. Brenda, do you want to stay on the golf course, or join me?"

"I'm with you, Jill; murder is so much more interesting than golf. See you men later." And the two women left in a golf cart.

They had time enough to change clothes when they arrived back at the suite. Right on schedule, the detective and Madison knocked on their suite door.

"Hello, Detective and Madison, what new information do you have for us?" Jill asked.

"It appears that the arsonist and murderer are not the same person, but they are closely related, like a mother and daughter, according to our crime lab. We're fortunate to have a state crime lab here in Asheville. It's the DNA from the fentanyl cellophane and the blood and hair DNA from the tree branch near your house."

"So, it could be the Williams/Monroe family?" Brenda said.

"I don't have confirmation of Ashley's travel plans," the detective said. "Also, we don't know what family the DNA belongs to—it's not in our database. Neither Ashley nor Mr. and Mrs. Williams have been fingerprinted nor had their DNA entered into any system."

"How about Ashley's real father or family? Could you make the link that way?" Jill asked.

"Ashley's mother is a widow, so short of exhuming her first husband, there's not much we can do."

"Did you look to see if Mr. Monroe was ever fingerprinted or had his DNA otherwise tested? I'll investigate that," Jill said.

"Why don't I look into that as I think we'll need to look at police databases," Madison said.

"Marie did a thorough search on Ashley Monroe. She is sure that Ashley has been in Hawaii since Saturday. You can be assured that it is accurate as Marie's sources are better than anyone's. That leaves us with Ashley as the primary suspect for the murder and her mother for the arson. Madison, let's go back to the driveway camera and see which two cars pull into the Williams' driveway and at what time. If we have eliminated everyone else and the killer had to use the road, is that enough for a search warrant to get a DNA sample from Mrs. Williams? Do you have the footprint identified as a women's shoe? Could we find Mrs. Williams buying two gas cans? Perhaps the cans might still be in her trunk. How about if we went back to Elder

Williams and ask for the recording for the night of Madison's house fire?"

"Surely Mrs. Williams isn't dumb enough to leave that kind of evidence around?" Madison said. "Do you think Elder Williams will be surprised by his wife's and stepdaughter's activities?

"You would be surprised at how arrogant so many criminals are—they think they are smarter than the police. I'll come up with a lie about a different crime as there's no reason to connect his driveway with a car needing to pass by it on the way to Madison's house fire. I'd like to get him without Mrs. Williams answering the phone," the detective said.

"Maybe you could swipe something out of the house that Mrs. Williams or her daughter uses," Jill said. "That's probably not legal, but at least we would get the evidence."

"It would be illegal for me to remove anything from their house without a search warrant," the detective said, frowning.

"What does Mrs. Williams do with her time? Does she volunteer anywhere that we could visit and get her sample? Surely, she does good works somewhere," Jill said.

"Did your friend Marie say if she volunteered somewhere?"

"Good question; let me take a look at what Marie sent. Just a moment," Jill said. "It says here that she volunteers at the Women's Society at the church. They meet on Thursdays at noon. There's your opportunity to run out to the house today since its Thursday. You just need to think of a different crime from the one you're really looking for."

The detective nodded, thought for a moment about other crimes in Asheville that he had heard about, and then made the call to the Williams household. He and Madison left a few minutes later, while Jill and Brenda headed to the police station to await the detective and the intern. An hour later they had sufficient proof to get a subpoena. They saw Ashley driving what turned out to be a car repair loaner heading into her driveway within an hour of Laura's estimated time of death, and she came from the direction of the church ruin, rather than from town. The night that Madison's house was set on fire, Mrs. Williams was seen leaving and returning in the middle of the night.

CHAPTER 25

With subpoena in hand on Friday, the detective returned to the Williams house where the CSIs and detective collected evidence of Mrs. Williams's DNA, as well as to Ashley's apartment, collecting hair from her hairbrush. Mr. Williams stood by watching with feelings of horror, disgust, and disappointment. He'd known within a month of his marriage to Cindy Monroe that it was a mistake.

She'd faked her interest in him and his church, as had her daughter. She wasn't the partner he hoped for to help him advance his church. After much discussion, he had convinced her to attend his church's stitchery group and she had done that faithfully, though he heard she routinely reminded the other women in attendance that she was the Elder's wife.

After they had the mother's DNA and it proved to be connected to the arson, helped by a scratch on her face from the tree branch she had left blood on, then the Asheville police called the Honolulu Police Department and had Ashley Monroe arrested and extradited back to North Carolina.

Elder Williams was mortified and knew he would have to move on to a new church. The shame and poor judgment that he displayed in bringing the Monroes into his life and this congregation were too much to overcome.

Jill, Nathan, Brenda, and Charles were celebrating the life of Laura Locklear and the end of a successful investigation. Brenda felt proud to have found the second footprint, giving her a small contribution to solving the case.

"Elder Williams isn't very alert to shady people," Brenda said.

"No, according to Detective Parnell, he was disappointed in himself as well as his wife and stepdaughter. He told the detective he was grieving for his first wife and feeling pressure to be married as the church leader. His decision-making led him astray. He'll be praying a long time to move beyond this episode in his life," Jill said.

"One good thing came out of this—for all his wife's demands to upgrade their home, the upgrade of the security system eventually led to the arrest and hopefully conviction of her and her daughter of their crimes," Nathan said.

A knock came at the suite door, and Nathan went to answer it.

"Hello, Stephen and Madison, we were just toasting Laura Locklear and the excellent detective work performed by some of the people in this room. And that includes you, Madison. I'll pour you a drink. Stephen, would you like one also?"

"That sounds great. I understand that you folks are leaving in the morning on an early flight. I have a proposal for Jill that we wanted to discuss."

"Yes, we are leaving early. Thank you so much for taking care of our rooms here. We had a wonderful wedding celebration and a successful murder investigation," Jill said.

"That's a great segue into my proposal. As you know, I adore my daughter and I want her to find an occupation that she's excited about. This hotel has been in my family for over one hundred years and I'm quite passionate about it. My daughter is from a new generation and wants to find her own way in the world. I want to help.

"So, here's my proposal. Madison assures me she wants to be a private investigator like you, Jill. She lacks training and experience. She has agreed to go to school and gain the education she'll need to get her license. Meanwhile, I'd like to bring you in as a partner for the next three years," Stephen said, holding up his hand to Jill as he guessed what her concern was.

"I don't mean to have you jointly occupy an office. Rather, I want to send Madison to you to understand your California office. Madison will provide free full-time support to all cases you have in the next three years. You in turn will serve as a telephone or video consultant for all cases that Madison has. You will be paid a stipend for that supervision that we can negotiate. How does this sound so far? Are you interested enough for me to continue?"

"Absolutely!"

"Once Madison has her license, I'll rent space in Asheville, and she can hang out her PI shingle." Madison rolled her eyes at that. "Further in Madison's future, she'll take over security for this resort and grow into a security and investigation firm."

"Madison, do you know why you want to be a PI instead of a cop?" Jill asked.

"I want the opportunity to pick and choose my work. I want to solve investigations without worrying about police rules. With a PI license, I have some legitimacy to question people, so I think that's the best alternative for me."

"Those are good answers. What made you so firm about this occupation?"

"The relief I felt when the Monroes were arrested. I could go back to my house and I have supreme satisfaction that the arsonist is sitting in jail. I want to bring those feelings to other people."

Jill nodded and said, "It sounds like you're making the right decisions for the right reasons. I'll help guide you for the next three years and you can work for me full-time from two-thousand-miles away. One thing you and your father didn't mention was self-defense. When Nathan came into my life and I was the target of thugs, he convinced me to pick a martial art. Nathan's a black belt in Hapkido, and I'm working on my blue chevron belt in Tai Chi. Nathan, when is the next martial arts convention in Sacramento? Madison, we'll want to take you to it and have you select and began to master one of the arts. As a PI, you'll get into some bad situations, and you can't count on having a gun or knife always available."

"That's an excellent suggestion," Stephen said. "I should have thought of it."

"No worries, we have that covered. Madison, if you come to California in the first week in December, we'll both be home and I'll oversee your martial arts education."

"I'll add you to the contract as well, Nathan. Thank you."

"There's no need to do that, Stephen. I enjoy sharing the martial arts with people and it brings me satisfaction to know I can help make Madison safer."

"One final comment, Stephen and Madison. You need to know that you'll get disrespect from police forces all over the world, and it will take you time to build a reputation as a competent investigator. You'll need to understand that going in. Also, being a PI is not necessarily a safer occupation than, say, being a crime scene investigator. Taking your personal security seriously and having an acute awareness of people at all times is critical to staying in the job long-term."

"I really do understand both of those issues. I heard some of the conversations about you at the station, but you've built up references that can't be ignored. I'll do that in time. I'll also research martial arts to see which one piques my interest. I'm happy you suggested it."

Jill stuck her hand toward Stephen and Madison and said,

"Deal." They covered her hand and repeated the words. Jill was excited to take Madison under her wing in the future. Her life was never dull.

An hour later, she was on a video call with Jo, Marie, and Angela to let them know the outcome of the case.

"I feel sorry for Mr. Williams, he must be crushed by what the women in his life did," Angela said.

"He was crushed and I heard he already resigned from the church," Jill said. "It was on the news, poor man."

"I for one would rather have my career crushed than live in the same house as my wife the murderer, and her daughter," Jo said. "They had to be awful people outside of these actions—you're not perfect in your personal life yet murdering on the side."

"That's so true. I have a call later with Henrik and I'll let him know about the conclusion to the case," Marie said.

"Thank him for his role in the case and for attending our wedding. I was going to drop him an email, after this call but I'll let you deliver the news in person."

They chatted a little longer about Madison's new role on the team. Jill wanted Madison to spend a day with each of them getting to know the service they provided for each case. Like Jill, they were excited to mentor someone new. They said their goodbyes and ended the call.

EPILOGUE

$\mathcal{J}$ill and Nathan were relaxing on a lounge with the wind whipping and the waves crashing in Half Moon Bay. A month after they returned from Asheville, they spent a long weekend at a nice coastal resort, soaking in the resort's spa and enjoying the relaxing sound of the waves.

"So we finally had our wedding night and there was no autopsy and no murder," Jill said.

"Yes, and we were by ourselves. The murder gods only line up work for you to do when the gang is all here."

"It's sad, but you're right. At least I'm going to have full-time help now. Madison arrives next week, and I'll take her through my lab and some of the local cases. I thought your suggestion of taking her to the martial arts convention was brilliant as she should learn some self-defense moves."

"Yeah, Stephen especially liked that suggestion. She's young and she needs to brush up on her people-watching skills to stay safe."

"She'll get some of that training as she works on her PI license, and I'll certainly work on that piece with her. I feel like

I'm mentoring a much younger sister to take on a new and dangerous role, but I really like inspiring the next generation."

"Do you think she'll stick with this occupation?" Nathan asked. "Her father is handing everything to her on a silver platter."

"I don't think any of us know if she'll stick with it. She's not flighty. She kept her head about her when her house was lit on fire. I like how her father could see the long game and down the road will give her the security of his resort to run as an extension of her private detective agency, or maybe the agency will be an extension of the hotel. Regardless, she has a bright future in front of her. You knew what you wanted to do from the beginning; I sort of did a mid-life career correction. If she stays with the security/detective field for twenty years and then pursues something different, then good for her. Maybe her close brush with the Monroes will keep her motivated."

"Yes, I agree with you. Did you hear what happened to them? Is their trial starting?"

"I read online that they tried to take an insanity plea, but no psychologist would certify that strategy so their trials will play out over the next year."

"I'm glad we were able to get some away time, and everything worked out in the end." Nathan handed a wine glass to Jill and picked his own up and they clinked their glasses.

"To you, Dr. Quint."

"I love you, Mr. Conroy."

"Okay you just scored points in your romance department bank account," Nathan said as they kissed to the sound of the soothing waves.

The End

ABOUT THE AUTHOR

I reside in Northern California with my rescue dog and cat. I love to travel, play sports, read, and drink wine and beer. I enjoy the diversity of the world and I'm always watching people and events for story ideas. All of my stories are generated by my imagination, I don't use AI to write books.

If you would like to sign up for my bi-weekly blog and announcement of new books, please follow this link: https://www.AlecPecheBooks.com

While you're waiting for the next story, if you would be so kind as to leave a review for this book, that would be great. I appreciate all the feedback and support. Reviews buoy my spirits and stoke the fires of creativity.

Readers that sign up for my blog receive a free prequel novelette for the Jill Quint Series.

ALSO BY ALEC PECHE

<u>Jill Quint, MD Forensic Pathologist Series</u>

Time's Up (prequel short story)

Vials

Chocolate Diamonds

A Breck Death

Death On A Green

A Taxing Death

Murder At The Podium

Castle Killing

Crescent City Murder

Sicilian Murder

Opus Murder

Forensic Murder

Return to the Scene of the Crime (short story)

Embers of Murder

Ashes to Murder

Mint Death

<u>Damian Green Series</u>

Red Rock Island

Willow Glen Heist

The Girl From Diana Park

Evergreen Valley Murder

Long Delayed Justice

<u>Michelle Watson Series</u>

Now You Don't See Me

Where Did She Go?

How Did She Get There?

<u>Dog Humor</u>

Eat, Play, Poop: Letters to my parents from camp

<u>New Urban Fantasy Series - Stephanie Jones</u>

The Awakening at Lake Tahoe (short story)

Witch's Medicine (2024)

www.ingramcontent.com/pod-product-compliance
Lightning Source LLC
Chambersburg PA
CBHW071803190726
48292CB00008B/2692